THE LADY GRACE
MYSTERIES

www.**randomhousechildrens**.co.uk

Also available in
THE LADY GRACE MYSTERIES series

THE LADY GRACE MYSTERIES

JINX

Grace Cavendish

Jan Burchett and Sara Vogler are writing as Grace Cavendish

RED FOX

THE LADY GRACE MYSTERIES: JINX
A RED FOX BOOK 978 1 862 30419 2

Published in Great Britain by Red Fox,
an imprint of Random House Children's Publishers UK
A Random House Group Company

This edition published 2008

13

Series created by Working Partners Ltd
Copyright © Working Partners Ltd, 2008
Cover illustration by David Wyatt

Set in Bembo

Red Fox Books are published by Random House Children's Publishers UK,
61–63 Uxbridge Road, London W5 5SA

www.**randomhousechildrens**.co.uk
www.randomhouse.co.uk

Addresses for companies within The Random House Group Limited can be found at:
www.randomhouse.co.uk/offices.htm

A CIP catalogue record for this book is available from the British Library.

Penguin Random House is committed to a sustainable future for
our business, our readers and our planet. This book is made from
Forest Stewardship Council® certified paper.

Printed and bound in Great Britain by Clays Ltd, Elcograf S.p.A.

For Bonnie and Ken Jay with love

The Daybooke of my Lady Grace
Cavendish, Maid of Honour to Her
Gracious Majesty Queen Elizabeth I
of that name

At Her Majesty's Palace of Whitehall,
Westminster

If you are not Lady Grace, then remove
your eyes from these pages forthwith!

The Twenty-fourth Day of August, in the Year of Our Lord 1570, St Bartholomew's Day

In my bedchamber after breakfast

I have a new daybooke and the perfect thing to write in it. This afternoon we are to go somewhere exciting!

At this moment I should be with the Court and entertaining our guests, but luckily I annoyed the Queen and she has dismissed me. Not that I meant to annoy her, of course. She is my favourite person in the whole world. Anyway, I only knocked a pile of books off a table – loudly – when trying to avoid a wasp, and everyone looked. As Her Majesty wants to make a good impression on our foreign visitors, she told me that my absence was more use to her than my presence.
I fled.

Mary Shelton is here too, having the final fitting to a dress that was one of Her Majesty's. She is concentrating on getting the sleeves shortened and will not mind me scribbling away.

It is often boring when we have visitors, and more than ever today. We are being honoured by a visit from Don Guerau de Spes, the Spanish Ambassador, and his retinue. At least, he believes he is bestowing an honour. A nuisance more like. What a stir his female relatives caused when they arrived yesterday, sweeping into the Queen's Presence Chamber in their fine gowns. They are an elegant flock and I saw many of the Queen's ladies stiffen at the sight of their splendour. The Queen favours the French fashion – and therefore so do the rest of us. This month, everyone wears the high-necked partlet with ruffs open at the throat. The Spanish ladies have no partlets at all but wear their gowns to the throat with uncomfortable ruffs right up to their chins. Many comments went buzzing around. The English ladies sounded scornful of all the finery, but as all the English gentlemen appeared to be bewitched by the black-haired beauties from Madrid, I think it was just jealousy! I had to hide my smiles at the daggered looks from Her Majesty's ladies.

I was not very interested. I was wearing my green gown with the ivy-leaf aiglets and was perfectly content. However, the most surprising thing happened: Lady Sarah Bartelmy did *not* join in with the scornful comments! She would normally be the first to condemn but she was quite silent. For a moment I could not think why.

But I quickly realized I was being a dolt! How could I forget that my fine lady has something other than foreign fashion to think on? The evidence was there, right in front of me, in the shape of Mr Daniel Cheshire. Sarah has eyes only for him. He is a member of the Queen's Gentlemen Guard and well-looking. He is tall, with reddish-blond hair. Some say he resembles the Queen's father, King Henry, when he was young and handsome. He is the eldest son of Mr Edward Cheshire, who is moneyed and high in the Queen's favour. So Lady Sarah's suitor has rank and wealth to boot (although he is the latest in a long line of flirtations for Lady Sarah and I doubt he will be the last).

This does not please our fellow Maid, Lady Jane Coningsby, who has tried in vain to get Mr Cheshire's attention. She needs little motive to fall out with Sarah. It does not help that Mr Cheshire barely seems to notice her, while his eyes follow Lady Sarah everywhere. And to rub salt in the wound, the other gentlemen of the Court, who would normally have fawned and flirted with Jane to kingdom come, seem besotted with our Spanish visitors. Jane is not the only lady of the Court to find this irksome. I overheard Lady Ann Courtenay in an aside to her neighbour.

'I wonder at our good honest English gentlemen,' she whispered. 'Having their heads turned by such black-haired ladies. They are not to be trusted, being foreign . . . and Catholic!'

Indeed, they are foreign *and* Catholic, and we are a good Protestant country, but I do not think our young men were too worried about that. Some were staring with their mouths open fit to catch flies.

I had plenty of time to inspect the Spanish ladies at the welcoming banquet last night. It was mostly a dull affair with many a long speech. Don Guerau's attempt at addressing the Queen was continually interrupted by his aunt, Doña Isabella de Spes. Doña Isabella is old, hairy and fat and seems to think *she* is the Ambassador. She would hardly let him speak without she must put in a comment. It was hard to understand her. She was speaking French, according to Mary Shelton, but her accent was so Spanish that I did not recognize any of the words except for *merrrrci*, where she rolled the 'r's fit to burst. Poor Don Guerau looked most uncomfortable! Doña Isabella seems to be in charge of the other Spanish ladies and they always sit meekly with their eyes lowered.

Her Majesty outshone them all. She was wearing a gown of gold with the narrowest of sleeves to make the greatest contrast with the huge sleeves that the Spanish ladies have. She looked so elegant.

I was very glad when the banquet and all the tedious speeches were over, and there was a performance by Masou and other members of Mr Somers's troupe. Masou may enjoy his position as one of the Queen's fools but I believe his greatest love is his acrobatics. He did four backward somersaults in a row, which drew many a gasp. I am very proud of him and wish I did not have to keep my friendship with him secret. It is the same with Ellie, my tiring woman. She and Masou will always be my best friends, but a Queen's fool and a tiring woman are not considered suitable friends for a Maid of Honour – although now that Ellie is my personal servant I can at least be in her company as much as I want.

A moment later

God's Guts! There was a thud on the chamber window that made me jump. It was a bird flying into the glass but it seemed none the worse for it and flew directly away. The bird has reminded me of the gift that Don Guerau gave the Queen on his arrival. Twenty beautiful white doves in five gilded cages. Her Majesty said she was delighted with the present and gave him a pretty speech in return. But I felt sad for the little white captives. I would rather see them flying free, as God intended.

But back to the banquet. When the troupe's acrobatics were over, Don Guerau made a deep bow to the Queen.

'Your Majesty,' he said, 'I have a boon to ask of you.'

He spoke in English, and Doña Isabella bristled like an angry bulldog that had had its bone taken from it. She clearly did not understand what her nephew was saying and therefore could not interrupt. Clever man, I thought. And I am sure I saw a flicker of amusement on the faces of her companions.

The Queen smiled but there was a guarded expression in her eyes. She must have been wondering what he was about to request.

'My kinswomen have heard of the famous fair of St Bartholomew,' he said. 'They have talked of nothing else since we left Madrid. We would be

greatly honoured if your beautiful ladies' – at this he inclined his head towards the Ladies-in-Waiting and Maids of Honour – 'would entertain them by accompanying them to the fair.'

My heart leaped at the thought. I have longed to go to the fair at Smith Field ever since I saw it from a distance once when I was little. It looked most exciting, full of bustle and noise, but the Queen has never agreed to us going. I found I was clenching my fists, willing her to say yes on this occasion, although I did not hold out much hope. Her expression was reluctant.

'It is not a place I would wish my ladies to go,' she began.

Mr Francis Walsingham, who was seated near her, seemed to put his hands on the table in a very deliberate way and the Queen immediately turned to him. She seemed to know that he had something to say. 'What is your opinion on this?' she asked.

Mr Walsingham is a close confidant of Secretary Cecil and Lord Robert Dudley. I find him rather scary. He is a secretive, black-haired, swarthy-skinned man who likes to wear dark clothing. He is soon to become Ambassador to the French Court but it is whispered that his main role for Her Majesty is as a spy. Mayhap his hands on the

table was a secret sign between him and the Queen!

At the Queen's request, he bowed his head. 'I believe Don Guerau has made a splendid suggestion, Your Majesty,' he replied. 'The fair is England at her most vibrant.'

The Queen held his gaze for a few moments as if reading a different tale from his words. Then she nodded. 'Very well, I give consent.'

At once the news flew between the ladies of the Court. I was not the only one who wanted to visit the fair, it seemed. And we are to go this very afternoon. I cannot wait!

A few moments later

Fran – one of the other tiring women – has gone in quest of some blue thread and Mary has taken the opportunity to tell me some gossip.

'Lady Frances Clifford told me that while we are at the fair, Mr Secretary Cecil is going to have the baggage of the Spanish ladies searched,' she said in a hushed tone, as if she thought someone would overhear. 'It is Mr Walsingham's idea. They will be looking for letters written by spies.

You never know when someone is plotting against Her Majesty. But tell no one, for it is most secret!'

I had to hide my smile – I had already heard this rumour twice since breakfast. First from Ellie, who had it from one of the Queen's personal servants. 'Most secret, mind you, Grace! Them Spaniards must never know.'

And then from Masou, who whispered it to me as an aside at the breakfast table. 'Most secret, Grace. Tell not a soul!'

Well, I shall not, but what good will it do as everyone seems to know?

I have little doubt that if we were to visit the Court of King Philip of Spain, then our luggage would also be searched. We are not great friends with Spain, for all Don Guerau's long speeches. I cannot think why. Yes, Spain is a Catholic country and we are not. And I suppose King Philip might still be cross that Her Majesty would not have him in marriage. (Mrs Champernowne, who has been Mistress of the Maids for ever, said he pursued her even before she was Queen and when he was still married to her sister!) And it is true that seafarers like Captain Drake are always robbing Spanish ships bringing gold from the New World. But Her Majesty does not punish anyone for it, so surely that must be a good thing to do – though perhaps the Spanish do not see it thus. Oh, and the Pope has excommunicated the Queen for not being of the true faith, as he calls it, so now any Catholic is allowed to kill her. Hmmm, perhaps there are reasons after all.

But how could anyone want to kill the Queen, the best monarch in the world and my own dear godmother? And yet it seems they do. Our brave Majesty has to be forever on her guard against other nations plotting her death. For did not my own mother die drinking poison that was intended for the Queen?

I would also give my life for Her Majesty – although I hope I never have to. And I will always be her Lady Pursuivant, thwarting any who would trouble her peace or put her in danger. Everyone knows that Mr Walsingham is her spy – but they have no idea of *my* secret job.

The chapel clock has just struck ten. I wish the time would go faster. I want to see the fair! We may be at odds with Spain but I am sure there will be no problems between the English and Spanish ladies this afternoon. After all, we are only going shopping, not to war.

On the Thames, about one of the clock

I will put first and foremost that I am writing this entry while sitting in a boat on the Thames. Otherwise I will look back at this in months to come and wonder why my handwriting was so messy. Suffice it to say, it is very hard to keep a neat script as our boat bobs and rocks. I had never given much thought before to the motion of a barge, but poor Lady Frances Clifford is greener than my old hunting kirtle! We had a hurried noontide meal before we left and I think she is about to see hers again. I cannot understand how she can complain of seasickness when we are not actually at sea, but it seems she can. She has a piece of ginger wrapped in linen pressed under her nose and is hanging over the side in a miserable fashion.

Yet I do not believe she is suffering as much as I am, sitting next to Lady Sarah. Daniel Cheshire, as the most senior Gentleman of the Guard present, has made sure he is in our boat and Sarah wishes to impress him. She is being a dreadful pest. She is between me and Lady Frances and keeps nudging and addressing me in fretful whispers: 'Lady Frances is sure to puke over my fine new silk skirt!' and: 'You will get ink on my sleeves, Grace!'

I was about to mention that if she kept fidgeting, this would certainly happen, when she grasped my arm – sending ink blots everywhere – and wailed in my ear, 'All this worry makes me frown and spoils my beauty. Mr Cheshire will never look at me now.'

If we do not get out of this boat soon, I might have to push her overboard.

I nearly forgot. Something very funny happened when we were in our bedchambers getting ready for our excursion – and it was all to do with Lady Sarah.

A cry of 'Thief!' suddenly shattered our peace. It came from the other Maids' bedchamber, so I threw down my quill and ran with Mary Shelton to see what was amiss. It sounded serious. I was picturing some burly knave making his escape laden with huge sacks of jewels. Instead we were confronted with the vision of Lady Jane glaring accusingly at Lady Sarah, who was glaring back. They were both as red as poppies and steaming like kettles. Carmina Willoughby and Lucy Throckmorton, who share the chamber with Jane, were cowering in the corner trying to keep out of the way. I wondered what Lucy might think – she is a new Maid of Honour and has not been at Court long.

'You cloud-brained clodpole!' shrieked Jane, her fists clenched. 'I did not give you permission to touch my salves and ointments.'

'But I only wanted a little of your face cream,' retorted Sarah. 'You never share so I had to take it!'

'It is my special salve,' growled Jane, 'and very expensive – though I doubt I shall ever use it again now that it has been tainted by your grubby paws!' And with that, she poked Sarah in the stomacher.

Sarah's eyes narrowed. 'How dare you, you gudgeon!' And she pulled Lady Jane's nose! Jane screeched at this, closed her eyes and started batting the air in front of Sarah's face. Sarah ducked behind her and pulled her hair. This made Jane shriek all the more. She reached for a bottle of perfume and threw it at Sarah but her aim was poor and it smashed against the wall. Sarah hunted around and grabbed a comb which she flung back. That missed too and flew out of the window.

Carmina and Lucy beat a hasty retreat to the door. The doorway was very crowded now. The tiring women, Ellie, Olwen, Fran – along with several Ladies-in-Waiting – had come to see what all the noise was about. It was as good as a play.

'Puts you in mind of the henhouse, don't it?' whispered Ellie to me.

'Jane, Sarah,' hissed Lady Ann urgently. 'Desist or you will have Mrs Champernowne to answer to.'

They took no notice.

'I know why you do not want me to have your stupid cream,' taunted Sarah.

'It is because it would be wasted!' growled Jane, snatching up a basket of hair papers to throw. 'Your looks are beyond repair!'

'Liar!' shrieked Sarah. 'It is because you are jealous of Mr Cheshire's attentions. Admit it!' She dodged and the basket hit the wall behind her.

Soon every pot in the room seemed to be airborne, and Jane and Sarah and the bedcovers and tapestries were covered in creams and salves and powders. We all flinched as a bottle of rose-water smashed against the doorjamb and sprayed over our gowns. We were quite wet – but smelled most fragrant.

Now it looked as if the fight must be over, for there were no missiles left, but Jane and Sarah now seized a pillow each and began belabouring each other over the head, screaming the while. At the door we all shouted encouragement – apart from Lady Ann, who covered her face with her hands.

'I wonder who's going to win,' Ellie said

wickedly in my ear. 'Shall we 'ave a wager?'

Suddenly the pillows split and the whole chamber was filled with a whirl of feathers. They slowly fluttered to the floor and there, in front of us, stood what looked like two giant white chickens, hands at each other's necks.

Ellie poked her chin in and out and made a soft clucking noise. This was too much for me. I laughed until my sides ached as Sarah and Jane tumbled over the beds, scratching and squawking.

'Methinks I have two more birds to be caged!' came a furious voice from the passageway behind us.

Horror! It was the Queen! We all fell to our knees in a squashed heap in the doorway. We had not heard her approaching, but with the mayhem in front of us we would not have heard the armies of Caesar himself! Jane and Sarah still had no idea she was there, for they just went on thumping each other. After what seemed like an age (it was probably about a minute really) they must have noticed that we were all on bended knee. Of course, I was not watching, for I had my head bowed, but the shrieking stopped quite suddenly and there was a sort of gulping sound (which was more like turkeys than chickens and made me want to laugh again).

I risked a peep. Sarah and Jane were hurriedly dropping into deep curtsies. Well, Jane managed a deep curtsy. Lady Sarah slipped on some spilled lotion and landed on her bum. I heard Ellie stifle a snort.

'This is not to be borne.' Her Majesty's tone was icy. She pushed us aside to enter the bedchamber. 'Is it not enough that I have to deal with the important matter of running this country and entertaining foreign powers? Must I also be treated to the spectacle of two of my Maids of Honour brawling like common drunkards? Nay, a common drunkard would not behave so low!'

She turned and glared at the spectators. 'I would refuse you all permission to go to the St Bartholomew's Fair this afternoon . . .' she said ominously (I held my breath), 'but I have already given my word to the Spanish ladies that you will accompany them. Therefore, go you must.'

And the Spanish trunks cannot be searched if we all stay here, I thought.

No one moved.

The Queen stamped her foot. 'What are you waiting for?' she demanded angrily. 'Go! Make haste to get ready.'

She did not need to say it twice. We fled!

And, amazingly, both my churlish ladies, Jane and Sarah, were clean and tidy in time.

And so now I sit in the boat and try to finish my entry. I am very pleased that Ellie has come with us and will see the sights of the fair. Since the Queen wants her Court to impress the Spanish ladies, Mrs Champernowne said we might bring all our attendants. Ellie is squashed in a corner but that is partly her own fault. She insisted on bringing a bag stuffed full of talismans, which seems to be taking up most of the room.

'There may be gypsies at the fair,' she warned darkly when I saw her packing her charms before we left. 'It's the sort of place those travelling vagrants go to sell their wares – and practise their dark arts.' She sorted through various herbs, a horseshoe and a stone which she has told me in the past is an elfshot.

'You will have no need of all that, I am sure,' I said.

'They were talking about gypsies in the kitchen.' Ellie sniffed at some basil leaves and thrust them into her bag. 'They have power over animals and plants. They can make them do anything they like. And they have their own strange spirit world – not the proper one like us. I don't know what manner of spirits they control but I wager there'll be evil curses involved so I'm not taking any chances.'

I do not think we are likely to encounter gypsies and I told Ellie so. It is against the law for such people to dwell in England and they risk death if they are found.

'Well, don't come running to me for charms when they turn you into a snake,' said Ellie firmly.

Hell's teeth! Lady Sarah has just flung her arm up to her forehead in a most dramatic way, causing me to splash ink on my sleeves. I hope Ellie has not noticed, for she will say it was no accident but a jinx. I will have to stop my entry soon anyhow. We are nearing our destination and poor Mrs Champernowne has begun to wring her hands. She is another one who is anxious about our expedition to the fair. Before we stepped into the boats she gave us dire warnings, her cheeks wobbling like jelly.

'You are not to wander off in that nefarious place, look you,' she said, wagging a finger. 'If it were not for Her Majesty's express wish, I would not go to Smith Field for all the silk in China. Keep a watchful eye for bankrupt nobles. I have heard dreadful tales of how they lurk in public places, looking for a rich lady to kidnap and make their bride.' This is her latest terror and she has filled our ears with her 'dreadful tales', so between her and Ellie one might think that St Bartholomew's Fair is a very dangerous place to visit. How exciting!

Six of the clock, before supper

Thank heaven I am not writing *this* entry in the boat. We are back and I have escaped to the Stone Gallery. It is quiet here and I need quiet if I am to remember every detail I have to record, for there has been a terrible tragedy and from that a mystery has arisen – one for the Queen's Lady Pursuivant to solve.

Our boat reached the steps at Blackfriars at last and we could see our horses waiting on Puddle Wharf. Mrs Champernowne looked as if her fears and worries were fighting each other to burst out of her ears. If she had had her way, I think she would have rowed us back single-handed to Whitehall rather than let us loose at the terrible fair! She saw me hastily cramming my daybooke into my penner and gave vent to a volley of tutting and shooing and almost chased me onto the bank. 'And don't be thinking you can run off on your own, Lady Grace,' she said through pursed lips. 'For whatever would Her Majesty say if I lost her goddaughter at Smith Field.'

There was a great commotion while everyone of the party found their horses. All the ladies sat behind grooms and we processed up St Andrew's Hill, the Gentlemen of the Guard riding ahead and behind. Along Ludgate and Old Bailey our horses could only walk in a single line, for the streets are very narrow. Even though I was impatient to get to the fair, I was glad we were going slowly. I wish I was a better rider, but I held my head high and tried to look as grand as our Spanish visitors. Wherever we passed, crowds stopped to stare at our dark-haired companions. I heard someone back off into a doorway, muttering darkly about foreigners. Then, at last, we were at the top of Giltspur Street and I could see St Bartholomew's Fair.

The whole of Smith Field was crammed with tents and stalls, bounded by houses on three of its sides and St Bartholomew's Hospital on the fourth. It was teeming with people. The air was full of the smells of ripe fruit and smoke rising from spit-roasted meat. We could hear the shouts of the sellers, telling everyone that there was no need to look any further, for their wares were best. I felt bubbly with excitement and the Spanish ladies were wide-eyed at the sight.

We dismounted and surged forward between the stalls in a bunch, thanks to Mrs Champernowne, who shepherded us all and muttered that she wished she had a sheepdog to help her. She did not seem to consider that we had plenty of men of the Court and at least twenty of the Gentlemen of the Guard with us – not to mention the Spanish guards (cleared out of the palace so that they did not see the search going on, I expect). I caught two of the Spanish ladies laughing at Mrs Champernowne behind their hands. How rude! It is all very well for us to make fun of our dear old Mistress of the Maids – a little, anyway, and only when she cannot hear – but other people should not do it.

I felt a tap on my arm and turned, thinking it was Ellie, but it was Doña Maria de Moncada Weatherville. I had spoken to her before. Her mother is English and she speaks both tongues perfectly.

'Do you think that is safe?' she asked, pointing at an entertainer surrounded by an admiring crowd. He was juggling knives and the blades were flashing in the sun. I wanted to laugh – Masou has shown me how a skilled juggler can make this look more dangerous than it is to attract a good audience who will pay well for the entertainment.

'I am certain he knows what he is about,' I assured her. Indeed he did. As he caught all the handles in his mouth, I heard many pennies being thrown into his hat on the ground! I wished Masou had been able to come to the fair. He would have loved the jugglers and tumblers, although I am sure he would have told me that none of the entertainers could hold a candle to him for skill. I was a little surprised that he had not joined our venture. He must have had something very important to do to miss this spectacle.

We walked on though the crowds. There were basket weavers, wood carvers, beer tents. I laughed to see the fortune-telling pig which, its owner was proclaiming, would answer important questions about anyone's future by giving one *oink* for 'yes' and two for 'no'. We walked down a row of stalls covered with bales of bright cloth and ribbon. Mrs Champernowne clucked fit to burst when the Spanish ladies wandered over to look at the silks and the rest of us gathered round the lace. She dodged between the two groups as if a dreaded impoverished nobleman were about to swoop down like an eagle and carry one of us off.

I felt something being pressed into my hand and jumped in surprise. I looked round to see Ellie closing my fingers round her elfshot.

'You startled me, Ellie!' I exclaimed. 'Whatever are you doing?'

'You'll be needing this, Grace,' Ellie whispered gravely. 'I've just seen something terrible!' She gave a nervous nod towards the crowd ahead and then looked away quickly. 'There was a foreign woman standing there, long dark hair and all, and she had an evil gleam in 'er eye. I reckon she's one of them . . . *gypsies*,' she hissed, then shivered. 'They'll curse you if they see you staring.' She suddenly dodged behind me. 'She's over there! Look, Grace! I mean, *don't* look!'

I suppose Ellie is right to be wary of gypsies. After all, everyone knows they are very mysterious and live secret lives that we know nothing about. Indeed, gypsies must be reported to the authorities if they are discovered. They are forbidden even to enter the country. Though I must admit that part of me was eager to see one – from a safe distance, of course – and I think Ellie was too. In spite of her words, her eyes were bright with excitement.

And, of course, when Ellie told me not to look it was the very thing I had to do, but I saw nothing dangerous. I took her gently by the arm.

'We shall be safe,' I said. 'The woman you saw was probably quite innocent.'

'Think what you will, Grace,' muttered Ellie, rummaging in her bag and wafting some garlic around. 'She won't come near us when she gets a whiff of this!'

'You will have no need of it, Ellie.' I laughed. 'Once she sees your fierce scowl she will take to her heels in fright!'

'*Hmph!*' grunted Ellie. 'How would you like to end up with boils . . . or a tail . . . or . . . or two heads!'

I pretended to think about this. 'Two heads would be quite useful, I suppose. Then I should spot you next time you creep up on me from behind!'

Ellie had to smile but she did not put her garlic away.

A lovely smell of fresh fruit reached us.

'Strawberries!' cried Lady Sarah, running over to one of the stalls. 'How I should love to taste them!'

We all followed in her wake. A tall man was standing behind his fruit, hands on hips. He did not seem to notice us at first. He had his eye fixed on a group of tents and stalls that stood a little distance from the rest, against the high wall of the hospital.

The tents were unusual, for they were shaped like domes.

The man suddenly noticed his noble customer and doffed his cap politely. 'Good day, my lady,' he said. 'I see a high-born lady like yourself knows fine strawberries when she sees 'em. You won't find better than Jacob Millerchip's. Ask anyone.' He held out a tray to Lady Sarah. 'I've got the juiciest peaches too, the tastiest plums, and the most delicate blackberries—'

'I will take a basket of these,' Lady Sarah interrupted, 'and none but the most ripe, for they are to be presented to Her Majesty' – she looked meaningfully at Lady Jane and muttered under her breath – 'as an apology for my part in the . . . disturbance this morning.'

Lady Jane scowled. She probably wished she had thought of it first. But Jacob Millerchip beamed at us all. He was delighted to hear that his fruit would soon be filling the royal belly.

'God's Life!' he exclaimed. 'The Queen herself eating my strawberries! You do me such an honour, my lady!' He made a great show of examining each little pointed fruit before laying it lovingly in one of his cone-shaped baskets. Then he put a pinch of pepper over for flavour.

'Let me settle with you for those, my man,'

Daniel Cheshire said, stepping forward with a handful of coins.

'You are too generous, sir,' simpered Lady Sarah. But I could see she was pleased, especially as Lady Jane was standing just behind her and had heard every word!

Jane waggled her head and fluttered her eyelashes in a good imitation of her rival, and I stifled a laugh.

'Where shall we go next?' Carmina wanted to know. 'I hope Mrs Champernowne does not think the food is poisoned here, for I am famished.'

'I should love to have my horoscope cast,' Mary Shelton said, 'but there are many fortune-tellers here today. It is hard to know who are true seers.'

'Pardon me, but you're right to be wary, my lady. Whatever you do, don't go near them lot over there,' Jacob piped up, pointing at the dome-shaped tents and spitting on the ground. 'They're cursed gypsies!'

At the word *gypsies*, Ellie gasped and Mrs Champernowne's lips tightened. An excited, fearful chattering ran round our party – and it must have been translated too, for the Spanish ladies were soon gasping and fanning themselves as nervously as the English!

'I knew no good would come of this accursed fair,' muttered Mrs Champernowne. 'If it is not noblemen it is ne'er-do-wells.'

'We don't want their sort here,' Jacob went on, 'putting hexes on innocent people and stopping us from selling honest wares with their trickery. If I could only find proof of their wicked ways, I'd tell the Clerk of the Fair about them.'

As he was speaking, a sharp little breeze whipped round the stalls, catching at our skirts and making the silks rustle. But then a truly strange thing happened. The breeze picked up and, with a sort of rushing sound, an icy gust whistled across the fair. I clutched hold of Mary Shelton and Ellie, for I could feel myself being quite blown away! It was most alarming. Our whole party was in a turmoil of flapping skirts and petticoats and the stalls around us rocked violently. Some were blown right over! Bits of broken wood tumbled over the grass among lost hats and nosegays. Jacob's stall collapsed in a heap and one of his baskets of blackberries fell in front of us. It rolled over and over and the fruit showered about our feet.

Lady Jane screamed at this – which was the most frightening part of the whole episode. 'Black fruit!' she gulped. 'And making straight for us. It is a sure sign of dark magic!' She checked that one of the handsome young courtiers was behind and ready to catch her, and then fainted clean away. She has that down to a fine art.

The wind died away as quickly as it had sprung up and we all started to rearrange our attire.

'Someone's after us, Grace,' Ellie hissed in my ear as she tried to pin my falling hair back up under my hat. 'Wasn't I right to bring my talismans?'

I could not think why anyone would bother to conjure up a wind to disarrange a few gowns and hairstyles. 'It was just a summer squall,' I replied. 'The worst that could happen is that Lady Jane will get blackberry stains on her white damask. Then her screams will deafen us all!'

Groups of grinning urchin boys had appeared from nowhere and were busily scavenging the scattered fruit. They were stuffing as much as they could in their mouths, while the stallholders were trying to save their wares.

'I've had enough!' cried an angry voice. I looked up to see Jacob Millerchip standing in the ruins of his fruit. He was red with anger. Bits of cloth, planks and broken poles lay at his feet, and some of his fruit was so squashed that it could not be sold now.

'I know who's sent this down on us,' he

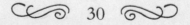

growled. 'It's those black-hearted gypsies. I'm going to see them. Who'll come with me?'

'I will!' cried someone.

'And me!' said another.

''Tis right clear it's that evil band,' piped up yet another. 'Look – their tents have not been touched!'

'Aye!' shouted several more, shaking their fists.

Soon a group of men was following Jacob towards the dome-shaped tents. I thought it was very possible that those particular tents had been sheltered from the wind by the wall of St Bartholomew's Hospital, but there would be no telling the angry men.

Everyone within earshot followed, and we were all caught up in the tide that surged after him. Even Mrs Champernowne could not keep us back, though she tried. And I can write here, where no one will see, that I was most curious to see these 'gypsies'. I had been told so many things about them that I think I was expecting monsters!

Of course, they were not monsters. A group of ordinary men and women were standing by their stalls and tents, staring at Jacob and his companions. They were dressed no differently from many at the fair, though their clothes were poorer than some. But they did have a foreign look about them. Their skin was dark, but not as dark as an African like Masou, nor olive like the Spanish, and they all had deep brown eyes. One of the women was with a black-haired little girl who gurgled and held her chubby hand out to Jacob as he strode up to them. The woman pulled her back.

A strong, thickset man came forward from the group.

'You conjured up that wind against us!' Jacob shouted at him. 'And we're going to make sure you're all arrested for it.'

The man looked puzzled.

'Don't pretend you know nothing about it,' sneered Jacob. 'You're all the same, you gypsies!'

The man stiffened and those around him shook their heads.

'You've no right to be here,' shouted one of Jacob's friends. 'Be off with you!'

'What have you got to say for yourselves, gypsies?' said another.

The thickset man held out his hands, palms up. 'We are no gypsies,' he said simply. He had an accent I had not heard before. 'We have done you no harm.'

This got the crowd muttering.

'Not one of your stalls was touched by the wind,' declared Jacob. 'Nor your tents. Don't try

 32

and tell me you had no hand in that.' He jabbed a finger at the man, who swiftly caught his wrist and held it in a strong grip. Jacob winced.

'You paid pickage to be at this fair – as we did,' said the man through gritted teeth. 'And that gave you the right to drive your stall poles into the ground. But you can't have sunk them in properly – as we did – so the wind took your stalls and not ours.' He released Jacob's arm in disgust and turned his back on him.

This was too much for Jacob, who leaped after the man with a yell and brought him down. In an instant, Jacob's companions had also gone on the attack and a horrible brawl had broken out! The so-called gypsy women swiftly vanished with the children into their tents.

I grasped Ellie by the hand and we tried to back away, but there was nowhere to go. The crowd was too dense. Daniel Cheshire snapped an order and some of the Gentlemen of the Guard moved forward to try to break up the fighting. The Spanish guards quickly surrounded their ladies. There were shouts and screams all around and more people joined in, some fighting, some trying to stop the brawl.

Suddenly I was whisked out of the crowd by Mrs Champernowne as if I was a fish on a line.

Ellie, who was still holding my hand, was dragged along behind me. Mrs Champernowne had somehow rounded up her other five charges and they were all huddled behind a tree.

'Get along there, look you, Grace!' she shouted above the noise of the mêlée as she pushed me into the middle of the bunch. Ellie squeezed in beside me, rummaging in her bag and pulling out a series of talismans.

'I do not think anyone will fight *us*!' protested Lucy, who wanted to see what was going on.

'Of course not,' Mrs Champernowne replied. 'But there will be a good deal of magic flying about. When those evil gypsies send their hexes this way, the tree will protect you, but if you see any whizzing along the ground, be sure to jump out of the way.'

I could not help thinking that the so-called gypsy men (for they had denied they were gypsies) were too busy fighting to cast spells – and the women had seemed more terrified than evil. But my companions looked at one another nervously, and Ellie tried to wave some basil in the air while at the same time dangling a protective pendant at her feet. She looked very awkward.

I peered out round the tree until I was told off for such folly by Mrs Champernowne.

'But if these people have such powers,' I argued, 'surely they could overcome Jacob and his men with one flick of a finger!'

That made everyone think.

'They are biding their time,' said Lucy wisely, and the Maids nodded.

'Did you see Mr Cheshire?' breathed Lady Sarah. 'He was so brave – he did not hesitate to act when the fight began. I do hope he comes to no harm.'

'Unlikely,' muttered Lady Jane in my ear, 'with nineteen other guards and all of them armed to the teeth in the service of the Queen.'

The fighting seemed to be expanding, and tussles were now breaking out near our tree. We quickly scattered as one of the gypsies landed in a heap at our feet. Now I found myself in a crush next to Doña Maria. She gave me a fearful smile. I wonder if she thought we behaved like this all the time in England.

Then, as suddenly as it had begun, the fighting was over. The two sides stood glaring at each other, while the Gentlemen of the Guard kept them apart, swords drawn. The fighters were sweating and out of breath. Some were bleeding.

The onlookers parted as a squat, pompous-looking man walked up to the battle scene. He was followed by a group of eager stallholders, who must have run off to fetch him, for they were all speaking at once, trying to tell him what had happened. The man silenced them.

'Who is that?' Doña Maria asked.

'The Clerk of the Fair,' answered Mrs Champernowne slowly and loudly. (She always speaks slowly and loudly to foreigners, as if they are stupid. She will not have it that Doña Maria speaks excellent English.) 'Very important man. He sort out gypsies. Hush, you! Now he speak . . .'

The Clerk addressed the brawlers. 'By order of Sir Robert Rich, owner of St Bartholomew's Fair and its lands, I command both parties to come without delay to the Court of Pie Powder wherein this matter shall be settled.' He glowered at the 'gypsies'. 'Shame upon you for such a display at a public fair.'

I thought that was unjust as we had all seen Jacob and the others start the fight.

'The Court of Pie Powder!' snorted Mrs Champernowne. 'Little good that will do. It only has the power to give them a fine or put them in the stocks! All very well if someone has stolen your gooseberries, but dark magic – now that is another matter!'

I thought that the Court of Pie Powder was

better than nothing. It meant that disputes taking place at the fair could be settled on the spot, even if the punishments it meted out were not so very fearsome.

The fighters on both sides brushed themselves down and trailed off after the Clerk, giving each other dirty looks. The stalls around us were being put back together. In a loud voice Mrs Champernowne was now trying to explain what had happened to our Spanish companions. I did not think she would notice my absence for a few minutes. After all, it would take her a goodly time to translate all that had happened into broken English! I took Ellie's arm and led her, in a roundabout way, nearer to where the 'gypsies' had made their camp. Ellie's eyes were everywhere, half in fear and half in excitement.

'Oh!' she said, all of a sudden. 'There's Lady Jane. What is she doing?'

Lady Jane was a little way ahead of us and acting most suspiciously. She was looking all about her – though she did not see us – and creeping along between the dome-shaped tents. It was so strange. I had thought her as scared of the 'gypsies' as everyone else, so what was she doing amongst them now?

And then I nearly burst out laughing, for

there was Lady Sarah, creeping along behind Jane –
in disguise! It was clear that she did not want Jane
to spot her. She was holding her skirts up to stop
them swishing and had a shawl wrapped tightly
round her head – to hide her bright copper hair, I
suppose. It was not a good disguise, for we knew
who she was straight away.

Every time Jane stopped, Sarah darted behind
something to hide.

Ellie grinned as we watched. 'Someone's
missing . . .'

'Who?' I asked.

'Mr Cheshire! He must be crawling about
somewhere among the tents. He's never far from
Lady Sarah's side.'

We giggled – quietly – at the thought of
Daniel Cheshire on his hands and knees, following
Sarah as she tiptoed along after Jane.

'What is Jane doing now?' I asked. Lady Jane
had stopped outside the smallest of the tents and
was glancing around furtively. Ellie and I quickly
slipped behind a stall of pots and pans and peered
through the wares to watch. To our astonishment,
Jane suddenly disappeared inside the tent.

Ellie drew in her breath. 'She should beware,'
she muttered, her grip tightening on the basil in
her fingers.

Sarah immediately scuttled up to the tent. She looked hard at it for a moment and then walked off with a very satisfied smile on her face.

'God's Oath,' said Ellie when she had gone. 'There must be something in the air. Everyone's gone woodwild today! What were those two about, sneaking round them gypsy tents?'

'I have no idea, Ellie,' I said. 'But I warrant it is something to do with their latest feud! Come, let us find the others.'

Ellie and I passed a stilt walker and two jugglers and came to a crowd buying hunks of spit-roasted boar. Ellie looked longingly at it, so I bought some and we shared it, wiping our greasy fingers on the little cloth the seller gave us. If Mrs Champernowne had seen us munching away, covered in fat, she would have had fifty fits!

'See that stall there,' Ellie said, with her mouth full. 'The one with moons and all on it? What does its sign say? Tell me, Grace.'

I looked. There was a brightly coloured tent a little way from us. Its cloth was covered with painted moons and stars and suns. A young woman sat in front on a stool, calling out to passers-by. She was pretty, with pale yellow hair trying to escape from under her cap, and she wore a medallion in the shape of a pentangle around her neck.

'It says *Palm Reading — Know Your Fortune*,' I read.

'That's just what I was looking for,' said Ellie. 'I'm going to have my fortune told like Doctor Dee does for the Queen.'

'But beware, Ellie,' I warned. 'We do not know if this woman is genuine. No one has recommended her to us. Doctor Dee is highly skilled or Her Majesty would not have him telling her when it is lucky to go off on progress and the like.'

'Her tent looks proper enough,' said Ellie firmly. 'It's got a pointy top so she's not with them gypsies. Don't be such a misery, Grace. If fortune-telling's good enough for the Queen, it's good enough for me.'

'Do you not fear that she might bring evil upon you?' I asked teasingly.

Ellie shook her bag of talismans. 'It'll be all right, Grace. I've got my charms. I'm going over.' Then she hesitated. 'As long as you'll come with me.'

'Very well.' I laughed. 'But don't believe all you are told!'

'Welcome, my ladies,' said the woman as we approached. She had a soft, floating voice, almost as if she were talking to herself. 'I am Sylvia.' She put her long fingers to her temples. 'I can sense that you need my help.'

'Not I,' I replied, for Ellie was tongue-tied. 'But my companion would like you to tell her fortune.'

'Then come with me into the quiet of my tent,' said Sylvia, and she led us inside and motioned for us to sit on a bench; in front of us was a table with all manner of herbs and protective amulets scattered upon it.

Sylvia sat opposite us. 'Tell me your name, mistress,' she asked.

'Ellie – Ellie Bunting.' Ellie faltered. I could see she was scared of this strange woman, even though she was so eager to have her fortune told. She fumbled in her bag. 'I've got my silver coin ready.'

'Then you must use it to make the sign of the cross on my palm,' Sylvia told her. Ellie did as she said. 'Now you are assured that there is no ill-doing here.'

Ellie seemed to relax at this.

'Show me your palms,' said Sylvia, holding out her own hands and taking Ellie's.

The fortune-teller gazed intently at them. She began to trace the lines on each hand with her long fingers. 'I can see you are a hardworking girl,' she said.

Ellie nodded.

'And that you work among the high-born.'

Ellie's eyes widened. She was impressed.

 41

'At the palace, I think,' Sylvia continued.

I felt a worm of disquiet. Anyone could tell these things from Ellie's rough hands and from seeing me by her side, but Ellie was entranced.

'A broad palm and slender fingers,' Sylvia went on. 'You are skilled in creating fine things with your hands—'

'I am an' all!' gasped Ellie. 'I fashion my lady's hair till it's beautiful – and that's not easy with *her* locks.'

'And you are musical too, playing the lyre or—'

'Well,' said Ellie, who cannot sing a note in tune and takes no interest in music, 'I've never had the chance – but I'm sure I could be.'

'And the strength of this line here' – Sylvia pointed to it – 'tells me that you are a quick thinker.'

Then her gaze became distant, as if she were seeing things far beyond us. I could see Ellie searching the fortune-teller's face to try and work out what she was thinking. Sylvia peered again at Ellie's palms, but this time she frowned and swayed in her seat.

'What is it?' asked Ellie, alarmed.

Sylvia made no answer. She grasped Ellie's hands tightly, gazing up at the Heavens, and her eyes rolled back in her head.

'Tell me!' Ellie demanded breathlessly.

Sylvia suddenly started as if in horror and thrust Ellie's hands from her. It gave me a terrible fright, but that was nothing to Ellie's reaction.

She shrieked loudly and jumped to her feet, knocking her stool over. 'What have you seen?' she cried. 'Tell me, quick!'

But Sylvia was shaking and her eyes would not meet Ellie's. She pushed the silver coin across the table to her. 'I cannot keep your money,' she breathed, and then, 'I am sorry. I am so sorry. Go, now!'

Ellie was pale as a ghost but she pushed the money back. 'I want to know what you saw.'

'You must leave this place and forget you were ever here,' whispered Sylvia urgently. 'I can say no more, not for anything, not if you were the Queen herself!'

'I'm not going,' said Ellie stubbornly. 'I'll not rest till I know – however bad the truth might be. Here, I'll give you more money.'

Before I could stop her, she plunged her hand into her bag and almost threw a handful of coins onto the table.

But Sylvia did not take any notice of them. Instead she studied Ellie's face intently. 'Very well, mistress,' she said at last. 'I can sense that you are of strong character and won't be denied. But I do this only to prepare you for your fate – and not for the payment.'

Ellie nodded and sat down again – but on the very edge of her chair so as not to miss a word.

Sylvia took her hand. 'I see that you will face a sickness. There is a break in your lifeline that tells me this illness will cause you pain – grave pain, the worst you could ever have!'

Her words sounded so sincere that I found my stomach tightening in fear for Ellie.

'What sort of pain?' Ellie managed to croak.

'In the belly,' Sylvia went on, in her quiet, floating voice. 'It is there that the pain will lie – and it will trouble you, mistress, and trouble you deeply. It may even—' She broke off, clasping a hand over her mouth as if to stop terrible words coming out.

I prayed this woman was wrong. I could not bear the thought of my friend falling ill – or worse.

'What can I do?' Ellie cried. 'Is there nothing that will stop it?'

'There is but one remedy,' said Sylvia gravely. 'It is the only one in the world that will save you.'

'Then tell me, quick!'

'Listen,' said Sylvia, leaning forward with her hands clenched earnestly together. 'You must seek

out the Miracle Lovage Remedy. Do not let false apothecaries sell you anything else. The remedy must be prepared in the right way, and in a true mixture.'

'But where will I find this remedy?' wailed Ellie.

'That will be hard.' Sylvia sighed, shaking her head sadly. 'But in this fair there are many apothecaries and many strange and rare medicines. Look carefully and you may find what you seek. But remember, you must ask for the Miracle Lovage Remedy and nothing else. And do it without delay. The ill fortune could come upon you swiftly.'

Ellie stumbled out of the tent as I hurriedly thanked Sylvia and ran after my friend, almost tripping on my skirts and the tent ropes as I went. I was further delayed by the crowd and thus lost sight of Ellie for a time. I believe I wandered round half the fair before I caught up with her at the last few stalls before St Bartholomew's Church. Her face was pale and tear-stained.

'I've asked everywhere, Grace,' she gasped. 'They've got lovage aplenty, but no one has the Miracle Lovage Remedy. If I don't get some soon it could be too late!'

I did not know what to say to her. It was dreadful to think of such a fate for my friend, even though I was sure it had come from Sylvia's imagination – at least, I hoped it had. 'Let me take you to see my uncle, Dr Cavendish, when we return to the palace,' I urged Ellie. 'Or to Mrs Bea, the wise woman.'

'No, it's the lovage remedy or nothing,' insisted Ellie. 'Why would that Sylvia tell me about it otherwise? After all, *she* wasn't selling it.' Her gaze was constantly ranging over the fair as she spoke. Suddenly her face brightened. 'Look, I haven't tried that stall!' she cried, and ran over to a nearby apothecary's stall, which was stacked with bottles of pills and potions and hung with good luck charms.

'Excuse me, sir,' she asked. 'I see you've got a lot of medicines here. I'm looking for a very particular one.'

The stallholder was a tall, fair-haired young man who gave us a dazzling smile. Such a smile would usually have had Ellie blushing, but today I do not think she noticed at all. 'Adam the Apothecary is here to serve you, my ladies,' he told us. 'I will help in any way I can, yet I cannot think what two such beautiful young ladies could need from me. It certainly cannot be my Secret of Everlasting Youth Cream. I am sure that looks such as yours will never fade.'

I sighed inwardly. I could tell that Adam was just trying to interest us in buying his cream. This trick probably worked on many young ladies – after all, it is not only Jane and Sarah who search for lasting beauty – but I believe that if he had truly discovered the secret of everlasting youth, he would not be selling his wares at St Bartholomew's Fair. Instead, he would be living in a large house with many servants – with a place at Court besides!

Ellie was becoming impatient. 'This is something much more important,' she said. 'I am looking for the Miracle Lovage Remedy. I have searched everywhere. Do you have any?'

Adam slapped his hand on his counter, making his bottles jangle. 'You need search no longer,' he laughed. 'I have the very thing!'

Ellie almost clapped in delight. Then her face clouded again. 'Was it made proper though?' she said. 'With the right things in it and all?'

'You are right to be cautious,' Adam said as he searched among his wares. ''Tis an ancient recipe known to few.' He picked up a small bottle of green liquid and held it up. 'Here it is – the Miracle Lovage Remedy. See the pure colour against the light?'

'How much?' Ellie asked. She looked desperate to get the bottle in her hands.

'Alas, my lady,' Adam replied. 'It will not be cheap, for it contains rare herbs from many lands.'

'I don't care how much it costs,' said Ellie, delving frantically in her bag for some money. Her face took on a look of panic and she drew me aside. 'I've no money left, Grace,' she whispered. 'I gave it all to the fortune-teller. Will you pay for it? I'll give it you back, every penny, I swear. I wouldn't ask you, only it might be life or death.'

There was something about Adam I did not quite like but I could not resist Ellie's pale, pleading face, and if by chance Sylvia were right, she would need this medicine.

'I will not hear of you paying me back,' I whispered to her. Then I turned to Adam. 'How can we be sure that we may trust you and that this potion is a true remedy?' I demanded.

Adam smiled. 'I understand, my lady,' he said smoothly. 'But can you afford *not* to trust me?'

Ellie clasped my arm. 'He has the right of it, Grace,' she hissed. 'Nobody else has the remedy. He is our only hope! *Please . . .*'

There was nothing more I could do. I squeezed Ellie's hand and told her I would buy the potion. Then I turned to give Adam his coins. He must have been sure we would make the purchase for he had already wrapped the bottle in a twist of cloth and was smiling happily at us. I paid him the money he asked for – it took nearly all my coin.

'And now we shall find Mrs Champernowne,' I said firmly. 'I have tired of this fair with its supposed curses and ill fortune.'

'But I'm so glad I spoke to that fortune-teller,' said Ellie, clutching the bottle of Miracle Lovage Remedy to her as if it were the most precious thing in the whole world. 'Think, Grace, if I had not been warned about this sickness, I couldn't've prepared myself!'

We walked up and down between the stalls looking for our party, and found ourselves once again close to the 'gypsy' tents. I was relieved to see some of the men who had been taken to the Court of Pie Powder back with their families. Then I caught sight of a familiar figure lurking behind their tents. What next? I thought. First Sarah and Jane, and now Jacob the fruit seller. Faith! It truly was a day for suspicious lurking.

Jacob looked angry. I was just wondering what he could be up to when Ellie caught my arm and led me over towards Mrs Champernowne, who was standing with Lucy, Carmina, the Spanish ladies and Daniel Cheshire.

'Make haste, Mr Cheshire,' Mrs Champernowne was saying. 'Look you find my other Maids.

They are lost in this terrible place!'

He had just made his bow to her when a cry went up.

'Fire! Fire!'

I turned quickly to see a horrible sight. One of the dome-shaped tents was in flames. It was the small tent that Ellie and I had seen Lady Jane slip into earlier. I stood there feeling quite helpless as men rushed to put out the flames, yelling to others for help. Soon the blaze was roaring, licking at the trees above. An old lady was helped out through the smoke. She was coughing and groaning and waving her arms in despair. Her rescuers sat her on a bench and someone put a shawl around her shoulders. The poor woman kept pointing back to the tent.

She was speaking in a strange tongue, but I soon knew what she was trying to tell us, for a man who was with her shouted, 'There's a Maid of Honour trapped inside!'

I gasped and a cold chill ran through me – it must be Lady Jane. We had seen her going into that very tent. I ran over to Mrs Champernowne, who was frantically checking her charges, but then I spotted Jane with Mary Shelton, making their way through the crowd to us – and now I knew who was missing.

'Lady Sarah!' I cried at the top of my voice. 'Lady Sarah must be in the fire!'

'God's Life!' Daniel Cheshire did not waste an instant. With no thought for his own safety he plunged into the burning tent.

Hell's teeth, I must stop writing, for I am called to supper ...

Later that night, after supper

I am in bed and should be asleep. Mary Shelton is already snoring. My eyes feel heavy and the flickering candle makes it hard to see, but I must persist. I have an important entry to make. Before I took out my daybooke tonight I said an especial prayer – for Lady Sarah's life has been spared and we are all more thankful than I can say! But I am sorry to have to write that she did not escape the fire unscathed. She has been badly burned and is in much pain. Poor Sarah.

When I wrote that I had been 'called' to supper, it was not quite true. I was chivvied and scolded to it by Mrs Champernowne as I did not stop writing the instant I heard her voice! (I do not blame her really. She is most upset about Sarah.)

So down I went to the Great Hall. It mattered not what terrible things had happened, Court life must go on and we must entertain our guests – although that was the last thing any of us wanted to do, I think.

There was a strange mood at supper. We were all shocked at the fire, but many were caught up in the drama of the rescue too. I could see that the Queen looked grave, yet she was as composed as ever and made sure that our Spanish guests were not ignored. They sat together looking sombre – more sombre than usual, I should say, for they are never bright and merry under the hawkish eye of Doña Isabella.

All around me I heard Daniel Cheshire's name being spoken. He truly was the hero of the hour. For no one could deny, not even Lady Jane, that he and he alone had saved Lady Sarah's life.

'I heard that Mr Cheshire found Sarah trapped by tongues of fire six feet high,' said Lucy in an awed voice. 'And that her scarf had caught alight.'

'It was that which burned her face,' added Carmina. 'What pain she must be in.'

'Poor Sarah,' Lady Jane breathed, sounding truly sorry for her fellow Maid. Their rivalry was completely forgotten. 'Her neck and arms were burned too.'

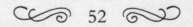

'I was told she was only saved from worse injury by Mr Cheshire's quick actions,' Mary Shelton put in.

'How so?' asked Carmina, agog. 'What did he do?'

'As soon as he found Sarah, he threw his cloak over her and smothered the flames,' Mary explained. 'Henry Westerland told me, and he had it from Mr Cheshire himself. He was so brave.'

'And so strong!' breathed Carmina. 'Did you see him carry her out through the smoke as if she were the lightest feather?'

'He will not take praise for it either,' said Lady Frances, who sat across the table from us. 'And he makes light of the burns he has to his own hands.'

'Indeed,' Lucy agreed. 'I saw someone trying to tend his wounds but he would have none of it. He did not leave Lady Sarah's side until she was brought safe to the palace.'

This was true. I do not think I shall ever forget Daniel Cheshire's face as he carried Lady Sarah onto the landing stage from the boat. He spoke soothingly, concealing from her the pain of his own hands, which I saw were raw and blistered. I believe he must truly love her – and I am coming round to the notion that this time she has a most worthy suitor. If he remains steadfast, that is.

I fervently hope that he does, for Lady Sarah's burns will surely scar, and a scarred Maid of Honour has little chance of making a good marriage. Sarah will be mourning her lost beauty. That was her great asset in finding a rich husband. She must wonder what will become of her.

Bowls of trifle were placed in front of us. The warm cream, flavoured with sugar, ginger and rose-water, is usually one of my favourites but I found it hard to eat any.

I could hear the strident tones of Doña Isabella, holding forth in a haughty manner. She spoke in French, and this time I managed to catch some of the words. I think she was telling those around her that such a thing as we had witnessed today would never have happened in her native Spain. The Queen caught every word, as of course she was meant to, I am sure, but being the great stateswoman that she is, she did not make a retort, even when the old crone turned and invited her to go and visit Spain for herself to 'see how calm and ordered our country is compared with the fights and fires you have to endure here'.

'I thank you, madame, for your kindness,' I heard the Queen reply in her perfect French, 'but I do not think I should enjoy the heat in your esteemed country.' She smiled and added in English, 'Which comes from burning so many heretics, methinks!'

I saw Secretary Cecil raise a worried eyebrow at the mention of how that Catholic country sometimes deals with people who are *not* of their faith. But I knew that the Queen would never have said it if any of the Spanish near her had understood.

'I hope you will consider my invitation,' Doña Isabella went on, thinking she was getting the better of the exchange. She turned a spoonful of trifle over in her plate and curled her lip in distaste. 'For you could taste the richness of our wines and wonderful foods.'

'I have no doubt of the superiority of your table,' said the Queen, in French again and with a gracious smile. 'For, my lady, I see in you one who has been lucky enough to enjoy its fruits to the full for *many* years.'

I wanted to cheer. The Queen was telling Doña Isabella that she was old and fat and the silly lady had no idea.

But my thoughts soon sped back to poor Lady Sarah. The talk around me had turned again to the fire.

'I warrant that fire was a gypsy curse,' said Carmina, with a frightened catch in her voice.

Several people threw salt over their left

shoulders at the mention of the word 'gypsy', to keep the devil from them.

'As was the wind that blew down the stalls,' put in Lucy knowingly.

More salt.

'The fire cannot have been a curse,' said Sir Pelham Poucher, waving his spoon at us. 'The old woman whose tent burned was one of the gypsies herself. Her tent was close by the others.'

'But the curse could have gone wrong and turned upon its creator,' said Lady Margaret Symonds, all low and dramatic, 'as well as upon Lady Sarah.'

By now such a quantity of salt had been thrown about that one of the servants skidded on it and fell over. So much for keeping bad luck away!

'That is the truth of it, I'll wager,' Sir Pelham said firmly, and slurped down his huge bowl of trifle.

'What can Sarah have done to bring such ill fortune down upon herself?' asked Mary Shelton.

'It does not take much,' Lady Margaret told her solemnly. 'You must be very wary around gypsies. Sometimes just a look or a word out of place will suffice.'

'That gypsy should be soundly punished for such a terrible thing,' exclaimed Sir Pelham, puffing out his immense belly.

'She already has been,' said Mary Shelton quietly. Everyone looked at her. 'Did you not know? She is dead.'

There was a gasp at this news.

'How can she be dead?' I asked. 'We all saw her stumble out of the fire. She looked shocked, but unharmed.'

'A rumour is abroad that she went back into her tent, though it was still burning,' Mary explained. 'She was mumbling about something precious that she must save. She was not seen again.'

'There is no better justice than that!' Sir Pelham brought his hand down hard onto the table. 'It saves the hangman a job.'

Most people seemed to agree with this. It was an easy solution to the mystery but it did not sit easy with me. One point in particular made me doubt whether the fire had been a curse gone astray, for if the old woman had meant Sarah harm, then why did she alert us all that a Maid of Honour was in the blaze? Besides, her distress at the time had seemed very genuine; no one had thought of that in their eagerness to lay the blame at the poor woman's door.

I have thought about this a great deal since supper, and I am now all the more certain that the fire was not caused by a gypsy curse. It *may* have been a mere accident, but was it not a great coincidence that the gypsy tent should burn down after all the ill feeling that had been stirred up against the gypsies? And besides, I saw the man, Jacob, lurking near the tent not long before the fire started. Could he have had something to do with it? Indeed, there is much that is suspicious about today's events. As the Queen's Lady Pursuivant, I think I must find a way to investigate and—

The Twenty-fifth Day of August, in the Year of Our Lord 1570

I am up with the sun and Mary Shelton is still
abed. I cannot believe I fell asleep halfway through
a sentence. There are the words unfinished and a
line of ink where my quill went limp in my hand.
This will not do. I could have got ink all over my
sheets and earned myself a scolding from Ellie. She
remembers her days as a lowly laundrymaid only
too well, and knows how long it takes to get ink
spots out.

The moment I awoke this morning I jumped
out of bed and dressed quickly in a simple kirtle. I
can manage the fastenings without bothering Ellie.
I felt she needed her sleep. I hope there is nothing
in this dire fortune told to her, but I intend to keep
a close eye on her health just the same.

My thoughts were full of the fire. Was it an
accident or not? If not, then we had witnessed a
murder! I itched to go back to the fair but I could
think of no good reason that I could tell the
Queen. I knew she would forbid me if I said I was
in search of a murderer.

Meanwhile I wanted to see how Lady Sarah fared. It was just past seven of the clock as I made my way to Mrs Champernowne's chambers, where she is being tended. There was the usual bustle of tiring women and servants in the passages but no one paid me much heed. I was very pleased not to encounter any ladies of the Court, for their foolish witterings about curses and gypsies make me want to throw things at them.

Sarah was awake and my heart jumped with pity at the sight of her. Olwen was helping her put a goblet to her lips. Sarah could not manage this alone with her hands so heavily bandaged. I watched her for a moment from the doorway. This was my first clear sight of her since the fire. Her face and neck on one side were badly burned. There were patches of skin that were red and raw and others that were bright pink. I could see fluid glistening on some of them as if they wept tears.

'How now, Sarah!' I said brightly. 'Here I am, up with the lark while you lie abed.'

She looked at me with eyes dulled by pain.

'It is good to see you, Grace,' she said drowsily. 'I am not much company. Your uncle has given me laudanum and I do not think I will stay awake for long. Better to sleep and escape this nightmare.' She raised her bandaged hands feebly in the air.

'Then I will be company for the both of us,' I told her. 'And tell you what occurred at the feast last night. Her Majesty had to put up with much from that old bat, Doña Isabella.' I tried to pull a face like the Ambassador's aunt by pretending I had sucked on a lemon. Then I put on a fussy Spanish accent. '*In Spain we have much better food and in Spain we have much better fashion and in Spain we fly in the air instead of walking!*'

'Indeed,' murmured Lady Sarah distantly.

I had hoped for at least a titter from her but I could tell she had not even heard my words. All the life had gone out of her. I felt truly angry. If someone had maliciously caused her pain and killed a poor old woman besides, I was determined to see them brought to justice.

But I knew I must first discover if the fire *had* been an accident. 'How did this happen, Sarah?' I asked gently. 'Did the old lady have a candle, or a fire in the tent?'

'She had neither.'

'Then how did the fire start?' I exclaimed. 'Did you see anyone?'

'No one,' Sarah replied weakly. I wondered if she was about to fall asleep when she painfully turned her head and fixed me with eyes brimming over with tears. 'Oh, Grace,' she sobbed. 'I am ruined . . .

ugly. No man will ever look at me now. I will never be able to marry. And then what will become of me – an old maid?'

I could think of no better future than to stay at Court, serving Her Majesty. It is what I intend to do. But I know that Sarah is like most of the other ladies at Court and longs for a good marriage and children. 'It will not come to that,' I told her gently. 'Your burns will soon heal. And it will be your choice to marry or not – although I would counsel you to stay single. The Queen will always give you a home with her.' I got up from the bed and went to the window. There was a cloth on the window ledge and I meant for Sarah to use it to dry her tears. 'Remember Her Majesty's wrath when Penelope Knollys wished to be wed. Would you really want to face that?'

At this moment I caught sight of Daniel Cheshire striding across the Privy Garden below, making for the staircase that would bring him to Sarah.

'Forget what I just said,' I laughed. 'I do not believe you will remain single for long, for here comes Mr Cheshire with a huge posy of cornflowers and goat's rue.' I was sure this would dry her tears but I was wrong.

'He comes out of obligation,' Lady Sarah whispered

with a pitiful sigh. 'He is too well-mannered to ignore my plight, but his visits are sure to dwindle when his duty is done.' She closed her eyes as if to sleep but tears seeped under her lashes.

'Nonsense,' I said gently. 'He comes now because he admires you, burned or no.'

She gave a tiny smile at that, but I had not said it merely to give her cheer. I now truly believe that Mr Cheshire is a thoroughly good and decent man. He would make Sarah a wonderful husband – if Her Majesty will agree. And I had to stop myself from laughing out loud at the picture of me, Lady Grace Cavendish, playing matchmaker!

Mr Cheshire was not to be Sarah's only visitor, for as I took my leave, I bumped straight into Mrs Champernowne and Lady Jane. Mrs Champernowne was too concerned with Sarah to scold me much and she bustled past with a platter of apricots and strawberries to tempt her patient.

I must have shown my surprise at seeing Jane, for she caught at my sleeve to keep me in the passageway outside the door.

'I am here because I feel that in some part this is my fault,' she whispered.

'How could you think that?' I asked in disbelief.

'Let me explain,' said Jane. 'Indeed, I must tell someone or it will fester inside me. I feel so guilty!

You see, Lady Sarah had been plaguing me to tell her the secret of my skin ointment. It is wonderful and keeps my face completely free of blemishes — while, of course, Lady Sarah does rather suffer with spots.' She paused and took my arm. 'I do not mean that in a bad way,' she went on hurriedly. 'But she and I do not always see eye to eye and I had grown weary of her constant badgering to reveal my secret. Mr Cheshire seems to like her more than me and so . . . I did not feel like telling her that my father gets the ointment from Rosa' — she gulped hard — 'the woman who died in the fire. He sends a servant to her regularly, so that my mother and I have a constant supply of the ointment, but my last pot was smashed when Sarah and I argued. And so, you see, I went to Rosa myself while we were at the fair. It seemed so fortuitous that we should be going there just when I needed more of my skin cream! But I think Sarah must have followed me — and that is why she was in Rosa's tent when it caught alight. Oh, Grace, if only I had *shared* my ointment with Sarah, she would not be lying here now, so disfigured . . .' By the end of this explanation, Jane's voice was halting and tearful. She seemed truly sorry for Sarah, and I wanted to reassure her, but before I could say a word, she choked back her sobs and went on into the chamber.

'Sarah,' I heard her say in a strangled, polite sort of voice. 'How are you?'

'Well enough,' was Lady Sarah's sleepy reply. 'Thank you for asking.'

It made a change to hear the two of them speaking civilly to each other. They always have some small argument between them. How sad that it has taken a tragedy to bring them to a kind of friendship.

Early afternoon

What a busy morning I have had and the day does not look set to slow down yet. I am in my bedchamber, and have just thrown on my riding kirtle, for I am about to visit St Bartholomew's Fair again – and with the Queen's permission, which I did not think she would grant, but, miracle of miracles, she did! Ellie is rushing about finding my boots and gloves and I am dashing off an entry while I can. I must record how I came to be going back to the fair. I should have time. Her Majesty has insisted that I go with an escort of Gentlemen of the Guard and they will take much longer to be ready than I will. So will the horses, for they must be groomed to perfection.

At last I can begin to investigate the fire properly: after all, little can be gained while I am cooped up here at the palace.

After I had written my last entry I went straight to the Great Hall, where breakfast had been laid out. I soon wished I had not! I sat between Lady Ann Courtenay and Lucy. It seemed that they had both had their fortunes read the day before. And I soon wished that *they* had not! My head was still full of the fire and the possible culprit so I was not in the best of moods for their silliness.

'See that servant,' hissed Lucy as a man brought more manchet bread to the table. 'He has a mole on his neck in the shape of the devil, and the teller told me to beware a squinting man.' She pulled a small cross from out of her sleeve and stroked it fearfully.

'There is no sign of a squint.' I laughed. I thought the mark looked more like a pig.

'How do you know he does not squint, Grace?' she said earnestly. 'We were all too busy looking at his mole. I will not eat that bread although I am still hungry.'

'And look at the goblet that holds my small

beer,' said Lady Ann, seizing the vessel and nearly splattering us all. 'It has a small crack in the stem. That is an evil portent, I am sure. Some danger is to befall us.'

'Yes,' I agreed, 'we are all to be drenched with your beer and will smell like a brewery the rest of the day!' In truth, I was a little disappointed that Lady Ann, who is usually a sensible woman, had succumbed to the general terror, and my words were perhaps sharper than I intended.

'Do not mock!' said Carmina from across the table. 'I saw three blackbirds and a sparrow as we came to the hall.'

There was a gasp from all the ladies present.

I was determined not to ask what on earth was wrong with that but she was determined to tell me anyway. 'It is a bad omen; I am sure of it,' she said. 'The blackbirds were a-warning of dark times ahead.'

'Dark times,' muttered Lady Frances Clifford gravely.

'And what of the sparrow?' I could not help asking. 'Does he counsel us to beware chirpy songs? Heaven forefend!' Really, I know there are true bad portents, but these were ridiculous.

'You do not understand,' Lady Ann said gravely. 'The lines in my hand told of something unexpected and the next thing I heard were poor Sarah's screams!'

Faith! These ladies were going to drive me bedlam mad! I pushed back my bench and went to leave. As I did, my crust of bread rolled off my plate.

'Another omen!' whimpered Lucy. 'We are heading for a fall!'

'Oh, terror!' shrieked Carmina – but not at Lucy's words, it seemed. She was pointing out of the window, a look of horror on her face. 'The portents were right,' she whimpered. 'Behold! A two-headed cat!'

We all looked.

'You are right,' I said. 'Two heads, attached to two bodies, eight legs and a tail apiece. It is just the two tabbies that serve as mousers for the kitchen. They are sitting close together, that is all.'

I left them to their bleating and was about to leave the Great Hall when Her Majesty came in. She would have normally breakfasted in her Privy Chamber but she probably felt she must show herself to her guests. The Spanish Ambassador and ladies sat together in one corner.

'Don Guerau,' said the Queen. 'I trust you all slept well.' The Spanish gentleman gave her a courtly bow and kissed her outstretched hand. 'I regret again that your relatives were exposed to the tragic events of yesterday.'

Don Guerau gave some reply and the Queen moved on.

I went to her and made my curtsy. She motioned for me to speak.

'I have been to see Lady Sarah,' I told her.

The Queen's face softened. 'Poor Sarah,' she said. 'Come, sit by me and tell me how she does this morning.'

'She is in pain, but my uncle has been tending her,' I said, deciding not to mention the visit of Daniel Cheshire. My hopes in that direction may come to naught so why anger Her Majesty with foolish talk of weddings?

'I wish we could find some way to stop her being permanently scarred.' The Queen sighed. Without thinking she touched her own face. Only a few of us know she has a smallpox scar there. The white lead hides it well.

Ah-ha! I thought. This is my chance. I will offer to go back to the fair to seek out an apothecary and investigate the fire at the same time.

But the Queen had other ideas. 'Perhaps Mrs Bea can help,' she said. 'Her skills as a midwife and wise woman are great. She is sure to have some salve or balm in her collection that will aid Sarah.

See to this for me, Grace, dear. Send your tiring woman to her.'

Mrs Bea is the wife of the Deputy Naperer and one of the kindest souls I know. I knew that she would be sure to help Lady Sarah if she could. 'May I go with Ellie, Your Majesty?' I asked. 'I would like to see Mrs Bea again.'

The Queen nodded her assent and I scurried off to find Ellie. At least I was doing something useful for Lady Sarah.

Ellie and I made our way through the Woodyard to Mrs Bea's lodgings. Ellie looked well enough and chatted away happily.

I was looking forward to seeing Mrs Bea. Funny to think that when I first met her last year, I thought I was going to see a witch. People whispered that about her because she is so skilled with healing, which is silly, for the round, twinkling-eyed woman is nothing like a witch at all.

We had not gone far when Ellie stopped and rubbed her belly.

'What ails you?' I asked. Ellie had turned pale. Was Sylvia's prediction coming true?

''Tis nothing,' Ellie said stoutly and walked on. 'I can just feel my breakfast moving about a bit.'

We reached Mrs Bea's door and Ellie rapped on the wood.

'Who's there?' called a voice from the other side.

'Lady Grace Cavendish and her tiring woman,' I replied. 'Come on the Queen's business, Mrs Bea.'

We heard a scuffling noise from within.

'I hope she is not tidying up on our account,' I whispered to Ellie. 'I would feel bad.'

At this the door opened and a beaming Mrs Bea greeted us, looking as round and comfortable as ever with her grey hair curling round her cap. 'Come in, Lady Grace, and dear Ellie,' she said. 'On the Queen's business, you say?'

Her chamber was extremely neat so she cannot have had much to tidy before she let us in. A table under the window was full of jars of herbs and ointments. Clean bowls stood stacked next to a pestle and mortar. She had small plants growing along the window ledge. I recognized most of them: basil, rosemary, fennel – ingredients she would need for her potions. Another door led to her bedchamber, I assumed, but that was shut. She stirred a steaming bowl that she had taken from her hearth as she spoke to us. Its aroma wafted around the room. It smelled foul!

'What's that?' Ellie gasped.

'It's a healing remedy for' – Mrs Bea seemed to

stop herself halfway through the sentence – 'a friend.'

I told her about Lady Sarah.

'I've heard about the poor Maid's predicament,' said Mrs Bea. 'And it is such a pity. I could have laid hands on a salve that worked wonders on burns – but, alas, no longer. I used to get it from another herbalist, a woman called Rosa. She came from the Orient lands and had balms and herbs you'd never see in England. They were her secret, of course, but she always shared the product of her recipes. She was at the fair yesterday and—'

'Was she the gyp— I mean, the woman that died in the fire?' burst in Ellie.

'Hers was the tent that burned down,' nodded Mrs Bea sadly.

I felt dreadful. The tiny flicker of hope for Lady Sarah had been snuffed out. Mrs Bea was looking towards the door of her bedchamber, deep in thought. And then, as if she had come to a decision, she turned to me.

'I have a secret to tell you,' she said in a whisper. 'Rosa did not die in the fire, although she was made sorely ill by the smoke.'

Ellie and I gasped at this news.

'But it is better that everyone believes she did perish,' Mrs Bea went on quickly. 'For a start people have been saying that Rosa is a gypsy, and

you know how dangerous that would be for her. But, worse, someone may have wanted to kill her by deliberately burning her tent.' She walked to the bedchamber door and put her finger to her lips. We joined her and peered in as she opened the door a crack.

There on the bed was an elderly lady, fast asleep. She had dark, deeply wrinkled skin and she wore a wool cap, although it is August and very warm. It was the woman I had seen outside the burning tent. I realized now why Mrs Bea had delayed opening her chamber door to us. She must have been hiding all trace of her patient.

'My husband found her at the fair,' explained Mrs Bea. 'He had come with his cart to buy bales of linen for new bedsheets and went to see what the commotion was all about. He slipped her away from Smith Field when everyone's concern was for Lady Sarah. We have known Rosa for years. She healed our youngest child when others had given him up. But I ask you to tell no one she is here. She doesn't have permission to be here on the Queen's land.'

Ellie and I promised without delay.

'The Queen's palace is surely the safest place for her,' I said.

At my words, Rosa stirred and opened her eyes.

She looked frightened at seeing strangers, until Mrs Bea told her that we were friends and sworn to secrecy. Reassured, Rosa tried to greet us, but her voice was painfully hoarse and the effort of speaking made her cough. With Ellie's help, Mrs Bea lifted her to a sitting position and brought in the foul-smelling brew.

'This will help with the smoke in her lungs,' she explained.

Rosa drank slowly. Certainly her cough was eased.

'How is the young Maid who was caught in the fire?' she whispered croakily.

I felt hope rising in my heart. If Rosa's first words were for my fellow Maid then she must be a kind woman, like Mrs Bea, and would surely help us with a salve.

'Lady Sarah's face is badly burned and she fears that she will be scarred for life,' I told her. 'Mrs Bea has spoken of your skill in these matters . . .'

Rosa took another swallow of the draught. 'I would normally have the perfect salve,' she said slowly, her accent dulled by the smoke in her lungs. 'Egg white and honey are good for soothing the pain and heat of a burn' – I saw Mrs Bea nodding at that – 'but to help healing and prevent scarring, it can only be . . .' She hesitated. 'I must ask you to keep this secret too – it can only be haoma.'

'What is that?' I asked.

'It is a very rare herb,' Rosa explained, 'and when the resin is added to a simple cream it will help burns to heal without any of the foul matter that can sometimes infect such a wound. I had only a small supply, but only a little is needed at a time. I would gladly have made some for the poor Maid, but I do not have it here.' Her eyes filled with tears and she began to cough. 'It was in a metal box,' she managed to say. 'I always dig a hole for it in the ground under my tent and then cover it with a rush mat for safekeeping. I do not know if it survived the fire, but there is every hope, for the metal of the box is strong.'

My heart leaped. Rosa's remedy sounded as if it was just what Sarah needed. It was possible that the resin was still at Smith Field, hidden in the ground in Rosa's secret place. As Her Majesty's Lady Pursuivant, I felt that it was my duty to go back to the fair and search it out for Lady Sarah. I was sure the Queen would agree – and that would give me a perfect excuse to investigate the fire as well. I had to get to the Queen without delay and ask for an escort, but first I needed to find out what Rosa remembered about the blaze.

'Have you any idea how the fire started?' I asked Rosa.

She shook her head. 'I cannot fathom it.' She sighed. 'I had no flame in the tent.'

My thoughts were interrupted then by poor Ellie, for she suddenly clutched her belly and bent over with a terrible groan. Then she clapped a hand over her mouth and bolted for the Woodyard. We heard her retching and I thought of Sylvia's prediction. Was it coming horribly true?

Ellie sidled back into the chamber, looking quite green. 'Forgive me,' she muttered. 'It's my ill fortune.' She told Mrs Bea and Rosa about Sylvia's warning. 'But I'll be all right 'cos I've got my Miracle Lovage Remedy. I should take some more . . .' She produced the bottle and pulled out the cork. She was about to take a huge swig when Mrs Bea put out a hand.

'May I see that?' she asked.

Ellie handed the bottle over. Mrs Bea smelled the potion, tasted a little on a finger and, without a word, passed it to Rosa, who did the same.

'Do not touch another drop!' said Rosa huskily.

'But it's the only thing that'll cure me,' Ellie protested. 'It's the Miracle Lovage Remedy that Sylvia said I needed.'

'On the contrary,' Mrs Bea told her. 'This potion has never seen a leaf of lovage!'

'Lovage can be very good for the gut,' said Rosa,

putting the stopper firmly back in the bottle. 'But unless I have lost all my skill, this is lobelia. A useful plant – if you need to vomit!'

Ellie frowned as she took this in, and then turned from green to red with rage. 'That Adam!' she shouted. 'He's a charlatan. He *made* me ill. He could see I was desperate so he pretended he had the Miracle Lovage Remedy. Miracle Hateful Remedy, more like!'

'Perhaps he hoped you would return and he could sell you another potion for your sickness,' said Mrs Bea. She sighed. 'Some call themselves healers that have no right.'

Like Ellie, I felt a surge of anger against Adam. He had tricked my friend and made her ill. I wished I had not let Ellie near his so-called cure. 'It is fortunate indeed that you came to see Mrs Bea today,' I said, taking Ellie's hand and squeezing it. 'You could have become dangerously ill taking that potion.'

'I'm very grateful to you both,' said Ellie, turning to Mrs Bea and Rosa. 'But what will I do? I was told I needed the remedy!'

'I will give you a lovage potion,' Mrs Bea promised. 'For now you truly need it to counteract the lobelia.' She fetched a small bottle from a shelf and held it out.

Ellie backed away.

'You are in safe hands now, Ellie,' I said. I took the bottle and pressed it into her hand.

'Have no fear, my girl,' said Mrs Bea with a smile. 'Mrs Bea's Miracle Lovage Cure will do just what it says.'

I was in haste to leave and see the Queen so that I could beg leave to go back to the fair, but I had to ask Rosa something first. 'What do you know of Jacob Millerchip?' I enquired. 'He seemed ready for a disagreement with you and your friends.'

'Ah, Mr Millerchip,' said Rosa, her voice no more than a husky croak. 'He came to me earlier that day wanting some of my burns salve. I asked him what it was needed for. I would never sell a potion without making sure it was the right one.'

Mrs Bea nodded. 'Look what's happened to Ellie,' she agreed. 'Giving out medicines carelessly can be dangerous.'

'I tried to tell him that,' said Rosa, taking another sip of her foul drink. 'But he got very agitated. He said it was no business of mine and that I should just give him the salve and be done with my questions.' She started coughing and Mrs Bea made her more comfortable on her pillow.

'I could see he was distressed,' Rosa went on.
'I tried to help him but he would not listen.
"You'll be sorry," he shouted, then stormed out
of my tent.' She lay back, her face grey with
fatigue.

This gave me food for thought. I already knew
that Jacob had a grudge against the so-called
gypsies and I had seen him skulking behind Rosa's
tent before the fire. Now it seemed he was eager to
get his hands on Rosa's remedy. This made him a
strong suspect. But why burn down a tent when
the very thing he was after might be destroyed?
Faith! I could not fathom his reasoning – unless he
knew that it was buried under the ground and
might not burn.

'We will leave you to rest,' I said to Rosa. 'I shall
go to St Bartholomew's Fair and seek out your
box. With luck it lies buried there still.'

Rosa's eyes lit up as if this was the best news she
had ever had.

'What is it like?' I asked.

'It is made of iron,' whispered Rosa. 'With a rose
etched into the lid.'

'Then I hope to return with it very soon,' I
said.

As we left, Mrs Bea pressed a small vial into
my hand. 'Burn this in Lady Sarah's bedchamber,'

she told me. 'It is geranium oil and has a calming effect. It will help her forget the horrors of the fire.'

I went straight to Her Majesty to gain permission for my venture while Ellie took the geranium oil to Lady Sarah, swigging her real lovage as she went. The Queen was in her Presence Chamber speaking to Don Guerau again. At least, *he* was speaking to *her*. It seemed to be a long and tiresome story about wine exports and I could see the Queen impatiently running her fingers up and down the string of pearls at her waist. She saw me and held up a hand to the Spanish Ambassador.

'Forgive me, Don Guerau,' she said, and I could hear the relief in her voice, 'but I believe my Maid has news of poor Lady Sarah.'

He bowed and moved aside.

'Has Mrs Bea supplied you with a cure for Sarah?' she asked.

'There is a possible salve,' I said, 'but the main ingredient lies in a box beneath the burned tent back at Smith Field.'

The Queen looked at me strangely. 'How would you know that?' she demanded.

I had not thought! Of course, I could make no mention of Rosa being at the palace. 'That is

where . . . I mean . . . that is what Mrs Bea told me. She gets it from that stall. And it is the only place. I pray you let me go there and search through the ashes in the hope that the box survived the flames.'

The Queen shook her head. 'I do not want you returning to the fair, Grace,' she said. 'It could be dangerous. We have had enough tragedy already. I will send one of the Gentlemen of the Guard.'

My quest looked hopeless. I wondered how on earth I could persuade Her Majesty to let me go. If she thought it was dangerous for me to dig up a box, how much worse would she think it if I told her I was playing the Lady Pursuivant?

'With all respect to the faithful Gentlemen of the Guard, My Liege,' I said instead, 'will they have the patience to carefully sift the debris? And' – I lowered my voice – 'Mrs Bea has told me that the ingredient is a secret, so I must keep her confidence.'

Her Majesty considered me for a moment. 'You are like a foxhound, Grace,' she said, 'ferreting out a cure.' Her eyes suddenly narrowed. 'As long as that is all you are after, my goddaughter.'

Thank heaven that was not a question, for what could I have replied?

'Well, you have my permission,' she said at

last. 'But how to explain your actions and keep them secret at the same time?'

An idea popped into my head. 'Perhaps Your Majesty would like me to return to the fair to pick out some fine cloth for you to give as a gift to your honoured visitors. There is little time, for the fair ends today, but one particular stall had beautiful silks. And you know you can trust me to choose well.'

'Hmmm,' said the Queen with a resigned smile. 'Perhaps not a fox*hound* but a cunning fox!' Then she raised her voice so that those nearby could hear. 'I would have you return to Smith Field this instant, Lady Grace. It is my express wish.'

I curtsied extra low to hide the excitement on my face. The Queen beckoned to Mrs Champernowne and began arranging my escorts. That is the only bugbear of the whole enterprise. I would much rather have sneaked back to the fair with just Ellie at my side, but such is the lot of a Maid of Honour.

I hear Mrs Champernowne calling to Ellie that the horses are ready. I must be off.

Evening, just after supper

We have finished supper and everyone is gone
from the Great Hall but me. The servants are
clearing away the trestle tables and I am tucked
away in a corner under a new tapestry that the
Spanish have given as a gift to the Queen. It shows
a daring rider on a very ugly horse. I am suddenly
put in mind of Doña Isabella – I know not why.

As soon as word was sent that the horses were
ready, I stopped my last entry, fetched Ellie and
made for the Holbein Gate.

'How are you feeling now?' I asked her as we
went across the Privy Garden.

'Well, my insides *were* much better,' Ellie told
me. 'That real lovage has done the trick, like Sylvia
said it would. But then you said we'd be travelling
on horseback and that was enough to send them
into a ferment again. I'm sure to fall off, and then I
don't know which'll be sorest, belly or bum!'

'You'll be riding pillion, Ellie,' I laughed. 'Behind
a groom.'

Ellie brightened at this. 'Cor, I hope he'll be a
handsome one to make up for my troubles!' She
grinned.

We were soon mounted and, accompanied by

four Gentlemen of the Guard, trotted down Whitehall. As a small party, we would make much faster time going by the streets and not the river.

Ellie was riding behind Tom Tufnell, who is ever so old – at least forty. She grimaced but then put on the comical air of a grand lady.

At the fair we dismounted. I thought of asking our escorts if they would care to take a drink, at my expense, in the Hand and Shears Tavern, but then I remembered that the Queen had told them to keep us always in their sights. And indeed they stuck to us like moths around a flame. I would truly have to show the cunning of a fox if we were to shake them off.

As soon as we entered the fair, Ellie spotted Adam, the apothecary who had sold her the fake potion. I heard her take a sharp breath. 'Won't be a moment, Grace,' she said grimly. 'I've something to do.'

I caught her arm. 'No, Ellie,' I hissed. 'I know you are angry with Adam but—'

Ellie shook me off. 'Make me puke, would he? I'm going to pull his nose from here to Christmas!'

I had a funny vision of Ellie in four months' time, a wassail cup in one hand and Adam's nose in the other.

'Think of Lady Sarah,' I reasoned, dragging her along through the fairgoers. 'If we do not hurry,

we shall be too late to find the haoma.'

I could see that the 'gypsies' were already
striking camp and leaving, even though the fair
would not be ending until late in the evening.
Luckily it looked as though the charred remains of
Rosa's tent had not yet been touched.

'Come, dear Ellie,' I whispered. 'We must reach
Rosa's tent before our eager protectors do – for I
do not want our guards to stand too close. I may
wish to speak to the people around.'

Ellie nodded and glared back at Adam. If there
had been any power in her looks he would have
dropped dead there and then. I kept up a brisk
pace, hoping the Gentlemen of the Guard might
dawdle. But they did not.

'Lady Grace,' called John Thornham anxiously, 'I
counsel you not to go near that area. So much ill
befell Lady Sarah there. And the silks are behind
us now.'

'You are right, Mr Thornham,' I replied. 'But
Lady Sarah lost a precious necklace somewhere
here and the Queen has asked me to search for it.'
I was pleased with my quick thinking. 'Pray stand
aside a little,' I counselled them all. 'I may soon
learn if someone found it – but people here will
not speak freely if they see Her Majesty's Guard
in earshot.'

'I am not sure, my lady . . . ' said Mr Thornham, shaking his head.

'We'll be all right,' added Ellie. 'We've brought charms.' She pulled out a handful of amulets and herbs. 'Don't suppose you gentlemen have got anything like that?' She looked at them each in turn. 'Thought not,' she finished triumphantly. 'Then you'd better stay back.'

'Well said, Ellie!' I congratulated her in a whisper as the young gentlemen shuffled awkwardly away.

I approached one of the 'gypsies', a pleasant-looking young woman who had been selling ribbons yesterday. All that was left of her stall was a basket of ribbons next to the piles of wood and poles. She was loading everything onto a cart, helped by a man and three skinny, dark-eyed children.

'Good day, mistress,' I said. 'May I ask why you are leaving so soon? The fair is not yet done and there are still many here to buy your beautiful ribbons.'

'We go because we are sad, my lady,' the woman told me, looking downcast. 'The fire yesterday – you must have heard tell of it – killed one of our . . . friends. Now we shall have a proper time of mourning.'

'No!' Ellie burst out before I could stop her. 'She's not—'

'Ellie is soft at heart,' I broke in, raising my eyebrows at Ellie to silence her. 'She cannot believe such a terrible thing has happened. Peace, Ellie.'

Ellie understood my meaning, for she fell silent and made sure she looked mournful.

I ached for these people and wanted to tell them that Rosa lived, but I had promised her and Mrs Bea. 'I am truly sorry for your loss,' I said gravely. 'It was a terrible accident.'

'Accident?' said the woman with a toss of her head. 'There are those among us who say the fire was no accident.' She caught sight of her children, who had tipped the ribbons out onto the grass and were now dancing with them. 'Stefan, Antoine, put those back,' she cried, 'or you'll feel my hand!'

'Who might have started the fire?' I asked quickly. 'Did anyone see?'

'No,' said the woman. 'Each man has his thoughts, though nothing can be proved. Now I must be about my business.' And off she ran to rescue her ribbons.

I was disappointed. I had hoped to learn more. We walked over to the blackened ground where Rosa's tent had stood. We kicked over the ashes and then realized we should be more respectful, for all around would believe we were trampling on Rosa's remains. It was soon clear that there was nothing to be found. I uncovered the hole in the ground, just as Rosa had described, but it was empty. Someone must have taken the box, for metal does not burn away completely and there was no sign of any remains. My thoughts were racing. Although there was still the smallest possibility that the fire was unconnected to the theft, I did not truly believe it. I was sure that someone had set fire to the tent to drive Rosa out so that they could steal her resin. They knew of the hiding place and would be certain that the haoma would be safe in its tin.

'I'm sorry for Lady Sarah's sake that we are unlucky,' said Ellie. Then she rubbed her hands together. 'But now there's time to see my friend Adam, after all,' she added.

'Not so fast, Ellie,' I instructed. 'We must go to see Jacob Millerchip now. He is the one most likely to have set the tent on fire. If he took Rosa's box, it may yet be hidden among his things. You talk to Jacob while I have a look around his stall.' I did not add that I also wanted to keep her at a good distance from Adam's nose!

'Very well,' muttered Ellie.

There were a few people gathered round the

stall and it looked as if Jacob had sold most of his fruit. I could not see the stallholder anywhere, but I bought four of the ripest peaches I could find from a shy girl who was sitting on a stool. She looked about ten years old, and had long auburn hair. I handed the peaches out to our escorts.

The Gentlemen of the Guard were only too happy to withdraw with their peaches. Like most young gentlemen, they are always hungry. They were soon more absorbed in trying to keep the juice from their livery than they were in keeping an eye on us, and I could speak freely.

I looked admiringly over the display. 'Truly, Jacob Millerchip has the finest fruit at the fair!' I said to the girl who had served me. 'Is he nearby? I would like to compliment him on pleasing the Queen so well with his fine strawberries yesterday.'

It was a white lie. Of course, Lady Sarah's gift for Her Majesty had been forgotten with all that had happened.

The girl blushed deeply. She seemed overwhelmed at being spoken to by one who came straight from the Queen. At last she replied, her face hidden by her curtain of hair. 'Father will be back anon, my lady,' she murmured. 'If you would wait, I am sure that . . .' She fell silent, I suppose thinking she had gone too far in telling a highborn lady what to do.

I smiled to ease her distress. 'It is no punishment to stand here and take in the wonderful smells of this stall,' I said. I waited while she sold some blackcurrants. 'And indeed, I cannot resist buying some of these greengages.'

The girl deftly filled a bag and took my money, looking around all the while as if willing Jacob to return.

'Your father must be proud of you being able to look after his stall so well,' I said. 'Tell me your name.'

'Abigail,' she replied, and then gave a cry as the wind caught her hair and blew it back. I saw a vivid purple scar running from her eye down to her lip. I was shocked – although I tried to keep it from showing in my face. But then my heart began to pound. I realized that I might have just learned of a motive for the theft of Rosa's precious haoma. I knew that Jacob had been eager to procure her salve and I could see now that he had good reason. He must have hoped it would heal Abigail's scar, for what father would not do all he could to save a daughter from being so disfigured?

'I am so sorry,' Abigail blurted out. 'I have offended your eyes, my lady.' She looked as if she would burst into tears at any minute.

I took her hand in mine. 'I am in no way offended,' I told her. 'Just sorry that you are so unhappy about your looks. You are very pretty. Indeed, you put me in mind of the Maid of Honour who was burned yesterday. Just like you, she will still be beautiful.'

Abigail looked relieved at hearing this, and pleased at being likened to a noble lady. 'Will she truly?' she asked, her eyes shining with hope. 'It was a terrible fire. I was so sorry that the dear old woman died.'

'What are you doing, wench?' came a man's deep voice; it startled us and had Abigail jumping from her stool. 'Gossiping instead of working? Fetch me some beer!' Jacob had returned. He thrust some coins into his daughter's hand but then bent and kissed her on the top of her head. She grinned and scuttled off to do his bidding.

The stallholder then remembered his manners. 'Apologies, my ladies. I hope Abigail wasn't troubling you.'

He wore a scarf around his neck although the day was hot. I wondered if he was sickening for something, or mayhap hiding some burns!

'No indeed,' I assured him. 'We were talking of the fire yesterday. Your daughter was saying how sad she was about the woman who perished.' I was quite pleased with myself for managing to bring the subject up so soon. I looked hard at Jacob, to see if his expression gave away any guilt, but he seemed merely morose and disinclined to talk.

'Brought it on themselves, those gypsies,' was all he would say. 'God's justice, I reckon. Pardon me while I serve this man here.'

He went to deal with his customer and I took Ellie aside. 'Can you distract him while I take a look around his stall?' I asked. 'A few minutes should suffice.'

Ellie nodded. 'I'll tell 'im about my grandmother who had the fruit farm!'

'You had a grandmother with a fruit farm?' I asked.

'Course not.' Ellie grinned. 'But he don't know that.'

I slipped round to the back of the stall where I could not be seen behind all the hangings. I could hear Ellie's voice, telling Jacob about her grandma's habit of singing to her gooseberries to ripen them, and how she always put badger droppings on her blackcurrants.

There were few places to hide anything. I spotted a pile of sweet-smelling trays which must have held Jacob's wares. They would be a good hiding place. I quickly glanced inside each one, moving them very carefully so as not to make a sound. Apart from a few squashed strawberries they were empty. There was nothing else to be seen. Then, just behind the trays, I spotted a large cloth sack, stuffed away as if someone had meant to hide it. The sack bulged. There was something inside. I glanced around to make sure no one was watching me. I could hear that Jacob was now being advised to pick his plums only by the light of a full moon.

With trembling fingers I loosened the rope tied around the opening of the sack, pushed a hand inside and found my fingers closing around a metal box. I pulled it out quickly and prised open the lid, not stopping to check for the rose engraving for I was sure it must be Rosa's. A strong smell of pepper filled my nostrils and I sneezed. Feeling very silly, I thrust the box back, clumsily tied the sack up and returned to join Ellie.

'Cover the roots with ten-day-old gruel, you say?' Jacob was saying to her.

'Not nine, nor eleven,' said Ellie firmly. 'You'll get better apricocks than you've ever seen in your life!'

'Ellie!' I said. 'Pray do not give away any more of your grandmother's secrets. What would she say? Come now, we must go.'

We took our leave of Jacob, who called out his thanks to Ellie.

 93

'You did well,' I said as we walked through the fair, our guards following.

'I enjoyed myself,' said Ellie. 'Did you find anything?'

'Nothing,' I told her wearily. 'We seem to be getting nowhere.'

'Well, I found out something,' said Ellie happily, taking a greengage from the bag she was holding and biting into it. 'Jacob was that keen to hear more about my grandmother I had trouble changing the subject, but I managed to ask him about his scarf, 'cos it's a hot day and all and it looked odd. Jacob said he got into a fight with one of the gypsy men, Yanoro by name.'

'Another fight?' I said. 'Were they stopped?'

'They were outside the fair,' Ellie went on, 'and it did not go to that Pie Crust Court, or whatever it's called. He put the scarf on so the gypsy didn't have the satisfaction of seeing that he'd hurt his neck. He showed me the bruises.'

'I wonder what the fight was about,' I said.

'Dunno,' said Ellie. 'But I do know this – Jacob said he would have got the better of Yanoro if the fire hadn't broken out and stopped them!' She took another greengage. 'So, if that's true, it can't have been him that started the fire.'

'*If* it's true,' I repeated thoughtfully. If it were

true that Jacob was fighting with a gypsy, outside
the fair, when the fire in Rosa's tent broke out,
then he certainly could not have been responsible
for starting that very fire. But I knew I would
have to investigate this alibi before I could believe
it.

I suddenly remembered that I must return with
the gift for the Spanish ladies and made for the stall
of which I had told the Queen. I ordered lengths
of a delicate blue silk painted with butterflies to be
sent straight to the palace.

Ellie stood by my side, munching through the
bag of fruit. 'These are good,' she said with her
mouth full. 'Try one, Grace.'

'No, thank you.' I smiled as we made to return
to our mounts. Ellie is always ready for food. I
suppose she cannot forget her days in the laundry,
not so long ago, when she never had enough to
eat. 'See, we are almost at the horses now. I shall
choke if I try to eat in the saddle.'

'A pox on it!' exclaimed Ellie suddenly. 'Now
I've lost my chance to speak to that Adam.' She
pursed her lips. 'You should've reminded me before
we left the fair.'

'I quite forgot!' I told her. It was true, I had. But
I should certainly not have reminded her even if I
had remembered. I thought that St Bartholomew's

Fair had witnessed enough fights without Ellie adding to them!

Back at the palace I went to find Mrs Bea again. It was possible that my main suspect had an alibi, so I wanted to see if Rosa might remember anyone else who might wish her harm or who had shown great interest in her resin.

Mrs Bea took me through to Rosa's bedchamber, asking after Ellie as we went.

Rosa was sitting up in bed, supported by a bolster. She was pale and weak but she smiled as I sat by her. 'It is kind of you to come and see me again,' she said. Her breath was a little laboured and I suppose I looked worried, for Mrs Bea came to my side.

'Don't alarm yourself, Lady Grace,' she said, taking her place on a stool on the other side of the bed. 'It's just the smoke and nothing worse. She'll be right in a couple of days.'

'I am happy to hear it' – I smiled at her – 'and would be happier still if the one who did this to you could be found, Mistress Rosa. I am sorry to say that I did not find your box,' I added as gently as possible. 'But I will not rest until I have. It is possible that Jacob Millerchip started the fire and stole the haoma, but he may have an alibi for when the fire began. Was anyone apart from Jacob unkind to you at the fair?'

Rosa wrinkled her brow. After a few moments she raised a gnarled finger. 'There was one.'

I sat up at this. 'Who was it?'

'Her name is Francesca. She is a very beautiful young woman, but sharp-tongued and always ready for trouble. She wanted me to prepare a mixture for her rival in love. It was to shrivel the drinker's skin and make her ugly and old before her time.'

'How horrible!' I gasped. 'What answer did you give her?'

'I told her no,' said Rosa. 'I never work in that way, doing ill to folk. Oh, but she wasn't having that. She bit her thumb at me and flounced off. But I know her well. She does not like to be thwarted.'

So this Francesca could be another suspect. 'Perhaps she sought revenge,' I mused. 'If she was willing to mar a rival's looks, who knows to what lengths she would go? Mayhap she thought she would burn your tent and steal your precious herb. That would be revenge indeed. I wish I could speak to her, but all the stalls around your tent were being packed up early. Your friends are in mourning for you. Indeed, I felt terrible for not giving them a word of comfort.'

Rosa gazed at me intently as if she could see right inside me. Then she took my hand in hers, and I could feel the hard, calloused skin of her palm. When she spoke, she had my heart racing with excitement. 'I have a secret,' she said in a low voice. 'And I can tell that you are one who will keep it close and not reveal it to a living soul.' I nodded silently. 'But you must swear on your allegiance to Her Majesty,' she whispered, her eyes suddenly sharp.

'I swear,' I said.

Rosa glanced about her as if fearful that someone might be listening. 'I have gypsy blood in me,' she said at last. 'My father was a gypsy and I was brought up to the life. All those who had their tents by mine are indeed gypsies too. We are proud of our birth but we must keep it a secret. Think of the lowest beggar in England and we are lower. They say it does not take much for us to feel the hangman's noose round our necks. So when Jacob and his friends declared us to be gypsies, we denied it.'

'If only I could go to your people,' I said. 'I could check on Jacob's alibi, talk with Francesca and, with your permission, give them the good news that you are alive.'

'There is a way,' said Rosa hesitantly. 'My people

always leave signs so that other gypsies shall know where they are.'

I leaned forward eagerly and Rosa drew shapes onto my hand to show me what the signs looked like. I hope I can remember them.

'I will find them!' I said, determined that I would do so, though not sure how I would be able to escape the palace.

At this, Rosa untied a charm that hung round her neck. It was a small curling shell, with a pearly lustre. She handed it to me. 'This will keep you safe, my lady,' she whispered. Her voice was quite hoarse now and it was difficult to catch the words. 'We believe that shells bring good fortune. It was made for me, and if you show it to my people, they will know you are a true friend.'

I took my leave, wondering why anyone could wish harm to such a person as Rosa. I had to find the gypsies – and tonight. Only they could confirm whether Jacob had indeed been too busy fighting to have started the fire. And if he had, then also with the gypsies lay my next suspect – Francesca. If she had been angry enough to set fire to Rosa's tent and steal the haoma resin, then mayhap she would still have it – in which case, perhaps I could yet help Lady Sarah by restoring it to Rosa so that the wise woman could concoct her healing salve.

But how to contrive my leaving Whitehall? I was chuckling to myself as I imagined the look on the Queen's face if I asked for permission to run after a band of gypsies, when I caught sight of Masou's livery of red and black velvet. He was just the person to help me slip out of the palace tonight. I ran to catch him up. Well, I did not exactly run, for that would have been undignified, but I still succeeded in catching my heel in a petticoat and nearly taking a tumble. So much for my dignity! But before I hit the grass I felt a strong hand on my arm and heard a voice asking if I had hurt myself.

'No, I thank you,' I mumbled. My rescuer was Daniel Cheshire. 'You are most kind, sir,' I said as I untangled my foot from the torn lace and made to continue my journey. 'I must not detain you further.' In truth Masou was disappearing round a corner and I did not want to lose him.

Daniel gave me a polite bow, but made no move to go. Instead he showed me a beautiful stomacher that he was carrying.

'You know Lady Sarah well,' he said in a rush, looking a little awkward. 'What think you of this? The work was done by Walter Fyshe, who makes many such for Her Majesty. Will the gift please her? I would not offend her for the world.'

I saw he had that look in his eye that Lady

Sarah's suitors often do – a sort of wistful look, as if she were a distant vision that he could not hope to reach. Usually I think that is just silly, but I was glad to see it in Mr Cheshire today. He could have sent a servant with the gift, but no, he was on his way in person. No matter what Sarah may think, Daniel Cheshire is not put off by her misfortune.

'She will be most pleased with it,' I said quickly, eager to get on my way.

'But I am worried that she may already have a similar one, and will not like to say,' the poor man insisted.

'I am certain she has not,' I assured him. It was true. Although she has practically ever other pattern under the sun, I had never seen her wearing one like this. It was a very fine thing – white satin with bone lace of delicate gold running down the middle.

But her suitor had not finished yet. 'Perchance another Maid has something like it?' he enquired.

I decided that Daniel Cheshire must know Lady Sarah very well if he had realized that she would not approve of that!

'You have chosen just the colour and pattern that she will most favour,' I said. 'And I have never seen such a one before.' Surely, I thought, there was no other aspect of the wretched garment that he could be worried about. 'And,' I added, to put a lid on the matter, 'if I am not mistaken she has the perfect skirt and sleeves for it. And now I bid you good day, sir.' I curtsied and made my escape before he could ask my opinion of the stuffing.

I walked quickly to the corner of the Banqueting House where I had last seen Masou. But he had gone and could have been anywhere in the labyrinth of Whitehall Palace. Hell's teeth, it was most vexing!

I returned to my chamber, puzzling over tonight's escapade, and found Ellie there. She was busily inspecting one of my skirts and tutting.

'How you get your clothes so dirty I do not know!' she complained, brushing as if she were beating a carpet. 'Looks like you've been rolling in the dust.'

'That is just the hem, Ellie,' I said. 'The ground has been so dry. Now, I have a problem—'

'And this?' Ellie pointed to a purple stain.

'A stray blackberry the other night at supper,' I explained. 'Listen, Ellie, I wish to—'

'And have you been stabbing yourself?' asked Ellie, showing me a gash in the material.

'It was done when I was embroidering,' I said. 'I was supposed to cut a thread but my skirt got in the way . . .'

'Of all the Maids I could have served, I got you.'
Ellie looked so comical pretending to be severe
with me that I hugged her.

'Come, Ellie, you would not want to be anyone
else's tiring woman,' I said. 'Admit it. For who else
would ask you to sneak out of the palace with her
on a secret night-time visit?'

Ellie looked curious. 'When?'

'Tonight,' I told her. 'Will you go with me?'

Ellie shook her head. 'I can't. I've promised to
help Mrs Bea prepare a special medicine for Rosa.
She needs me to collect some fresh mallow. Then I
am to help in the preparation, for she said it would
be long and complicated and I am just the quiet,
patient sort of person she needs by her side. Those
were her very words,' she added proudly as I raised
my eyebrows. 'Where will you be going anyway?'

'To see the gypsies,' I said, and Ellie's eyes
widened.

'No, Grace,' she said in a low voice, as if they
might somehow overhear her. 'Don't get caught up
in all that . . . magic and so on.'

'I have to, sweet Ellie.' I shrugged. 'And I have a
talisman so they will know me for a friend. But I
am glad that, although you think me a messy Maid,
you are still concerned for my welfare.'

'Huh!' said Ellie with a twinkle in her eye. 'Your

welfare? It's your clothes will suffer if you go chasing after gypsies!'

'Then worry no more,' I said. 'I shall not wear my own clothes. I must travel as a peasant. And for that I need you to work your own magic and conjure me up some rough weeds from somewhere.'

'I shall find you Masou too,' said Ellie firmly. 'For I'll not let you go alone.'

'Thank you, Ellie,' I said. 'So you *are* concerned for me after all.'

'No,' said Ellie. 'But if anything happens to you, I might be set to work for Lady Jane!' And she waved her brush at me and swept out of the room.

'Good luck with your search for Masou,' I called after her, 'for I have found that quarry very hard to pin down! I wonder if he is now working for the man in the moon for all that we have seen of him lately.'

I sat on my bed, thinking about the night ahead. I had to find out from Yanoro whether he had indeed been fighting Jacob when the fire had started, and I needed to speak to Francesca — tactfully, for it sounded as if she could be a woman who would stop at nothing to get what she wanted. Yet I could not do any of this if I did not find a means to leave the palace unobserved, *and* I needed a horse to take me on the journey. Supposing, like Ellie, Masou could not help me. I would have to go alone. I felt a thrill of fear run up my back, and a soft tap at the window had me leaping to my feet, my heart pounding wildly.

'Grace!' Masou's head appeared at the glass. I was so relieved to see it was him that I nearly flung open the casement and sent him plummeting down to the ground! I composed myself and unlatched it a crack. I should not have been surprised to see my friend – he has climbed taller and more precarious walls than the mere thirty feet to my window.

'You gave me a fright, Masou!' I exclaimed crossly.

'Alas,' sighed Masou, flapping away a nosy pigeon. 'I thought you might give a warmer welcome to a friend who has made this effort to visit you.' He indicated the ground, a long way down. It made my head swim.

'Of course I am glad,' I said. 'But I hope no one has seen you.'

'I am invisible as the air itself!' declared Masou. 'Ellie said you have a mystery to solve. She garbled something about the fire and Lady Sarah. Speak. How can I help?'

I told him of my suspicions and my need to find

the gypsies – but I told it all very briefly, for I was scared that he would lose his grip and fall at any moment.

Masou nodded. 'Leave it to me. I shall meet you at nightfall at the Bowling Green. That is' – he gave a cheeky grin – 'if I do not fall. *Aaargh!*'

His head suddenly disappeared and I shrieked aloud, threw open the window and leaned out. He had surely gone to his death. But there he was, curse him, curled up on the ledge. I slammed the window shut, but could still hear the wretch chuckling.

In faith, both my friends are striving to get the better of me today! If I were not so busy, I swear I would be planning my revenge.

Tonight, as soon as Mary Shelton is snoring, I shall fashion a blanket into my shape under the bedclothes so that no one knows I am gone. It has served me well in the past. Oh dear, I feel sleepy – but that may be because I ate so well at supper. The chicken pie was too delicious to resist a second helping. I pray I shall stay awake this night.

The Twenty-sixth Day of August, in the Year of Our Lord 1570

Early morning, before breakfast

Lack-a-day! I have had precious little sleep and my head is spinning. Here is Mary Shelton, slumbering peacefully in her bed, and how I yearn to do the same. But I must not – else I shall forget all that has happened this past night. I have found out some interesting things that could prove important. Hell's teeth! I am still dressed in my rags. Mary would have a fright if she awoke and saw me thus.

A few moments later

I am in my nightgown now – and feel even more like sleeping. I have stuffed the old clothes I wore under the bed and must remember to tell Ellie. If they are left too long I believe they may crawl out on their own! Also, I suddenly thought to take the

Grace-shaped bulge out of my bed. All is well and I will make a start.

Last night, Ellie sneaked into our chamber as soon as she heard Mary Shelton's first snores. She thrust a pile of rough and smelly clothes at me and I pulled off my nightgown, which of course I had been wearing to show Mary I was going to bed, and put them on. It was so dark that the skirt was pulled on back to front and the chemise inside out, but with Ellie's help and some silent giggling, I was finally ready. Then Mary muttered some nonsense in her sleep, sending us into fits. We had to run so as not to wake her.

Ellie walked with me through the endless passageways of the dark palace. We avoided the few people still around and kept to the shadows, for I looked very ragged. When we stepped outside, I saw with relief that there was a full moon and no clouds. We darted in between the trees by the Bowling Green. Ellie left me at the Holbein Gate.

'Don't let them gypsies put a curse on you,' she said as she pressed an amulet into my hand and disappeared into the shadows.

I heard the sound of hooves approaching and the dark shape of a horse and rider appeared. I confess the apparition was a little ghostly until I saw it was Masou, riding a rather bedraggled donkey.

'Greetings, fair one!' he said, holding out a hand to me. 'Let me carry you away on my noble steed. We shall go to lands afar, to many a strange sight and magical—'

'Nonsense, Masou!' I interrupted as I was dragged onto the beast behind him. 'Your noble steed does not look as if he could carry us past the Holbein Gate, let alone to lands afar! Where did you get him?'

'Her!' said Masou. 'And not so loud. You will offend Elizabeth.'

'Elizabeth?' I nearly exploded with mirth. 'Is this donkey named for the Queen then?' I held my nose. 'She does not smell as fragrant.'

'Her real name is Moll,' Masou confessed, urging the donkey into an ambling walk, 'but she is fiery and stubborn so I call her after Our Gracious Majesty.'

'She looks neither fiery nor stubborn,' I giggled.

'Wait until we are beyond the gates,' said Masou. 'She is a different animal once she smells freedom.'

I had to stifle my chuckles and avert my face, for we had arrived at the gate. I knew that the alarm would be raised if a Maid of Honour was seen being carried away on the back of a donkey – even so royal a donkey as Elizabeth.

'Good even, sirs,' Masou called chirpily to the guard. 'I am on a special errand. It is most secret.' I poked Masou in the back. Surely he was not going to tell the guard where we were going!

The guard nodded, looking interested.

Masou lowered his voice. 'There is a man in London who is most merry in his ways,' he said solemnly, 'and I am off to ask him for some new jests with which to amuse Our Gracious Majesty.'

'That is very well,' said the guard doubtfully. 'But need you take the girl too?'

'Indeed I must,' said Masou, 'for she is a solemn and miserable wench and only the most comic of japes will raise a smile in her. If they please her, they are sure to please the Queen.'

The guard waved us through.

Masou was right about our mount. Elizabeth had, I swear, only got her front hooves onto the road when she brayed, kicked up her heels, nearly throwing me over Masou's head, and charged off. I clung like a limpet to Masou, wincing with every step of her clumsy canter, for she wore no saddle!

As we bumped along, I explained in jolting breaths that we had to follow signs to the gypsies' camp: they would start at Smith Field, so that was where we must begin our quest. 'And where have you been these last few days?' I asked, but the teasing boy would not tell me.

'Like you, Grace,' he said, 'I have matters to deal with that I cannot tell a soul – not even you. All will be revealed soon.'

With that I had to be content, although I was itching to know more.

We dismounted at the site of St Bartholomew's Fair, which was empty of stalls now and looked strangely quiet in the moonlight. The grass was flattened and ragged and strewn with old food and broken boxes. We led the donkey through the field to where the gypsies' tents had been.

'Rosa said her friends had left signs so other gypsies could follow,' I told him, treading carefully over the moonlit grass.

'Where are they, Grace?' asked Masou. 'I can see nothing but broken sticks.'

'Broken sticks they may be,' I said, 'but look at the way they are stuck in the ground. That is one of Rosa's signs. It points north.'

'It is the only clue we have,' Masou muttered. 'Let us take that path.'

As if she agreed with us, Elizabeth pawed the ground and *eeyored* loudly.

We scrambled onto her back and had soon left

the narrow streets of Clerkenwell for the dusty tracks between fields and farms, finding signs to follow just as Rosa had told us we would. I admired the way the gypsies communicated secretly with each other, for no one would see their signs if they did not know what to look out for. Some were etched into a tree or onto a large stone, but all were very clear when we looked diligently.

We came to the milestone for Canonesbury village. I found an arrow in a circle, scratched into the earth, pointing off the road and into the deep wood.

As we neared the trees, Elizabeth came to a sudden halt and we nearly went tumbling. I was glad to dismount; the ride had been so uncomfortable. I now realized that although my riding kirtle is thick and heavy, it would have cushioned my bum far better than the thin garb I was wearing! But now, however hard Masou pulled her or slapped her rump, Elizabeth would not move forward. It was very dark in the wood beyond and I began to wonder whether she had sensed something that we could not. I could hear rustling, and strange calls – most likely foxes or badgers, I told myself, but my heart quickened its beat all the same. Thinking back, I am sure it was just the excitement of coming so near to our goal.

Masou must have seen something in my face for he laughed. 'A-feared, my Lady Pursuivant?' he said as he tethered Elizabeth to the nearest tree. 'If you will go chasing after your suspects at night, you must expect a little darkness!'

'A-feared?' I snorted. 'Fie on you, Masou. I was simply wondering where this camp can be. There is no sign of it yet. Come, follow me.'

I strode off with a determined step and Masou had to catch me up. Soon we had tall trees close on both sides and the way was too dark for all but a little moonlight. Then we entered a copse of birch trees. Their slender silver trunks stood out boldly. Beyond was a clearing. It was lit eerily by the moon, the shadows of the trees around making odd shapes on the grass at our feet.

As we stepped into the clearing, we were suddenly surrounded by tall dark figures. There had been no sound, no movement that I could tell, but there must have been at least ten or twelve of them and they all carried heavy clubs. The hairs stood out on my neck as I grasped the shell Rosa had given me. Were these the gypsies? I certainly hoped so.

'Who comes here?' growled one of the men, in the strange foreign accent that I had heard at the fair.

I could not help trembling a little, but spoke up as fearlessly as I was able. 'We come as friends.'

'Friends!' spat another of the men. 'You are not one of us.'

'Dirty *gaujos*,' put in another, 'who creep upon our camp by night to burn down more of our tents.'

They advanced towards us, wielding their clubs. They looked very fierce with their long wild hair and dark staring eyes.

'For the love of Allah, show the shell, Grace,' urged Masou, 'or we are lost!'

I quickly held it up high. 'I bring this sign that I am your true friend!' I squeaked.

The men murmured together in their strange tongue, and the clubs were lowered. A tall, broad-shouldered man stepped towards me, pulling the shell roughly from my hand. Another figure arrived with a flaming torch. He thrust it in our faces, and the men looked us up and down, while their companion examined the shell. I remembered him from the fair. It was he who had enraged Jacob Millerchip by telling him that his stall had blown down because he had not dug the poles in properly.

'This shell belonged to . . . she who has died,' he growled. 'How did you come by it?'

 114

'Rosa is—' I began, but was immediately silenced by horrified cries around the group.

'Speak not the name of the dead!' shouted the tall man. 'You will bring her *mulo* – her spirit – down upon us.'

'But Rosa is not dead,' I insisted. 'She is being well cared for. She gave me the shell so that you should know I come from her.'

All the men began to crowd round us and talk at once.

'Rosa is not dead?'

'We must go to her.'

'Where is she?'

'We cannot take you to your friend,' said Masou. 'Rosa has asked for her place to be kept secret. But be sure she will return as soon as she is strong.'

The tall man pressed Rosa's charm back into my hand. 'For this happy news I thank you. You are truly friends of dear Rosa – and so you are our friends also. I am Gunari. Come now and meet my people.'

Masou looked among the trees, as if trying to see where the people could possibly be, and Gunari laughed. 'We gypsies are masters of silence and stealth. We are welcomed nowhere so we hide ourselves well. Follow me.'

They took us deep among the trees. At last we

saw the flickering lights of torches and could make out the silhouettes of many people gathered in a large clearing. One of our escorts shouted something in which I only caught the word 'Rosa', but suddenly they were all leaping to their feet, whooping and clapping. Some began to sing. I could see how dear Rosa was to her fellow gypsies, even though she was only half joined in blood to them.

Masou and I stood in the middle of the throng. Some of the gypsy women clasped our hands, others cried for joy. The children skipped about and even the tiny ones who could not understand were infected by the happiness around them. The horses tethered to the trees nearby tossed their heads wildly. I was pleased to see that Elizabeth was amongst them, enjoying a good drink and a feed. She looked very meek and mild now – not at all like the obstinate beast who had refused to go another step for us.

Soon a bright fire was crackling and some of the gypsies took up a dance. It was an amazing sight – as magical as the Court masques that Masou and the troupe perform for the Queen.

The flames from the fire lit the clearing as the dancers whirled around, flinging their arms in the air. The women wore brightly coloured dresses, and scarves round their hair with coins dangling from them. They jangled as they moved, for bracelets covered their arms and chains swung from their necks. Everything sparkled in the firelight. Not one of them had dressed in this gypsy garb at the fair, I remembered. It would have betrayed their true identity straight away.

All at once Gunari called for silence. 'We must eat!' he announced. Some of the women went off to their carts, but one as old as Rosa approached us, wrapping herself in a patterned shawl.

'I am Barbara,' she said, in a heavy accent. 'Come, sit by the fire while the feast is prepared. You will eat with us. When one of our people dies, we eat nothing for a long time, for we are very sad that evil death should take away someone dear to us. But now we can break our fast.'

'We shall be honoured,' said Masou, with one of his flourishing bows. But before he could sit with us, a group of noisy boys took him by the hand and pulled him away. I sat with Barbara on some blankets.

'I thank you for coming to give us such glad news of Rosa,' she said. 'Few *gaujos* would think to do such a thing for those they call gypsies.'

'What is a *gaujo*?' I asked. 'One of the men called us that.'

'All who are not of our people are *gaujos* to us,'
explained Barbara. 'Now tell me, how is Rosa?'

This gave me a perfect opportunity to find out
more about the fire. 'She is recovering,' I said, 'but I
find it hard to think that anyone would wish to
harm such a good person as her. There was a
stallholder near her tent just before the fire. His
name is Jacob. Did you see him perhaps?'

Barbara's eyes narrowed. 'I know the man you
speak of,' she said. 'Yes, which of us would not
remember him at that fair? Jacob stirred up hate
towards us. One of our men fought with him.' She
called to a curly-haired young man who was
adding wood to the fire. 'Here, Yanoro, that *gaujo*
you fought with at the fair – could he have burned
Rosa's tent?'

Yanoro flung the last log onto the flames so
angrily that it sent sparks high into the air. He
strode over to us and held out two large fists. I
could see that they were cut and bruised.

'This is what I did to that insect!' he spat. 'He
frightened my sons when he threatened our
people, and anyone who does that will answer to
me. I dragged him from the fair and frightened
him back. I would have done worse, but as we
fought, I saw the flames from the fire and knew
that I was needed.'

So Yanoro was making much of his fighting skills, just as Jacob had. I could see that his face was badly bruised too and he walked with a limp, so Jacob must have landed a good few punches of his own!

'So Jacob could not have started the fire,' I said.

'He hates us enough to do it,' Yanoro growled, 'but in truth I know he could not have. We were fighting long before it began.' He turned away curtly. 'I must tend to my horse.'

'Yanoro is still angry,' said Barbara. 'He is wary of all *gaujos* and finds it hard to speak to you.'

'I understand,' I replied and looked around for Masou. My friend was in his element, surrounded by a crowd of boys. One of them was standing – or rather wobbling – on his hands, and Masou was holding his legs. The others cheered and laughed when their friend collapsed in a heap, and then clamoured for a turn. I took my leave of Barbara and went to Masou's side. I had to seek out my next suspect, Francesca, and from what Rosa had told me of her, I did not want to speak to her alone.

'My friends are able pupils,' said Masou as soon as he saw me. 'But they have a lot to learn before they can do this!' He flipped nimbly back onto his hands and then over onto his feet again. He bowed while the boys clapped.

'I am sorry to drag you from your performance,' I said, 'but I need your help. There is someone I must find.' Masou looked disappointed. He obviously did not wish to leave his admiring audience. I knew just how to win him over. 'No matter,' I said breezily as I walked away. 'I shall find her by myself. I simply have to look for Francesca, a young and very beautiful woman who—'

'Wait for me!' cried Masou eagerly. I chuckled to myself as he made his excuses to the disappointed boys. Then he set them juggling with sticks, which put the smiles back on their faces, and caught up. 'Young and very beautiful, you say,' he mused. 'I shall seek her out for you in no time!'

And he did. After a few enquiries, we were directed to a girl a few years older than me, perched on one of the empty carts near a group of tethered horses. She had her head bent over a bracelet which she was twisting in her fingers.

'Francesca?' I asked.

The girl raised her head. I saw Masou's jaw drop open – she was indeed beautiful, with long thick black hair and arched eyebrows. I found myself wishing that my mousy locks were more like hers. I wondered how this girl could possibly need the aid of potions to find a suitor!

'Who's there?' Francesca asked sharply. We had our backs to the fire so our faces were in shadow.

'Good even to you,' I said. 'We are Grace and Masou, the ones who brought you news of Rosa.'

She jumped off her cart and looked hard at us. 'Ah, yes,' she said. 'Dear Rosa, I am so fond of her.' There was something in her voice that made me wonder how sincere she was being. 'I expect she has spoken of me.'

I took a deep breath. Francesca was not going to like my reply. 'She told me you had an . . . argument, over a potion to give to a rival in love. She said she would not let you have it.'

Francesca's eyes flashed. 'I have done nothing bad. I only wanted to make sure that it was I, and not Sabina, who won the heart of Tomas.'

This was interesting. I had not accused the girl of anything and yet she was very quick to defend herself. Had she got something to hide?

'Do not fear,' simpered Masou. 'I think my friend may have misremembered the story.'

Francesca smiled sweetly at Masou and he almost melted on the spot. I gave him a dig in the ribs. This was not helping my cause! I wanted Francesca to tell us more of the argument.

'But you must have been very cross that Rosa would not let you have the potion for which you asked,' I persisted. 'Anyone would be, do you not think so, Masou?'

'Huh?' Masou grunted from the depth of his daze.

'Did Rosa say that?' sneered Francesca. She paced up and down, waving her arms as she spoke. 'Well, what if I was? She had no reason to deny it to me. And I would have paid her. Why is she spreading rumours about me?' Then she stopped and shrugged. 'The fire has addled her wits, poor thing.'

Masou watched her, completely enchanted. I could see that this hot-headed young woman was used to getting her own way. But how far would she go to achieve her ends?

She stopped defiantly, hands on hips. 'Anyway, I don't know why Rosa is so troubled about it,' she said, and now there was a triumphant smile on her lips. 'In the end I had my prize without her help. Just after I'd spoken to her, Tomas came to me. "You look even more beautiful when you're angry," he said. And he gave me this. It was his grandmother's.' She showed us the bracelet on her wrist. It was a delicate silver chain with a charm in the shape of a beetle. 'We are to marry very soon.'

I am sure I heard a soft groan of disappointment

from Masou, which made me want to laugh. But then I reflected that I had lost another suspect. Surely Francesca would have forgotten her anger towards Rosa when she had suddenly become engaged and would have no reason to burn down her tent. Now I had no leads at all!

I smiled. 'We wish you luck,' I said. It will be Tomas who needs the luck, being married to her, I thought to myself, but I added, 'So, for you, the fair was not all disaster . . . ' hoping to glean more information from Francesca.

'No, indeed, it was the best day of my life,' she replied. Perhaps she saw a touch of disapproval in my face (certainly not in Masou's, the noddlehead!), for she hesitated. 'Aside from the fire, I mean.'

'Can you think of anyone who would hate Rosa enough to try to kill her?' I asked.

'No gypsy would do such a thing,' answered Francesca. 'But I do remember one other trader at the fair who was jealous of Rosa – for she's known as a fine herbalist and healer and did much better trade than him – and he behaved very badly towards her.'

This was rich, I thought, coming from someone who had behaved very badly herself. 'What did he do?' I asked.

'I saw him standing a little way from her tent on the first morning of the fair,' said Francesca. 'When anyone went to buy from her, he would shout out loudly that she was a fake and he had much better wares. Most took no notice – I think many knew Rosa and her skills – but he led more than one person away from her and off to his own stall.'

'Do you remember his name?' I enquired hopefully.

Francesca thought for a moment. 'It was Adam,' she said at last. 'He called himself Adam the Apothecary.'

Adam the Apothecary! I was thankful Ellie was not with us, for she would have shrieked to the Heavens at the mention of that dreadful name. As it was, I could hardly contain my excitement. I had a new suspect, and a strong one at that! Had Adam set the fire? Had he heard about the precious haoma resin hidden in her tent and decided to take it for himself with no thought for the loss of life? It was possible, but where would I find him now that the fair was over?

A call went up – the food was ready. Francesca took us by the hand and led us back to the fire. A cheer went up at our arrival and platters of meat and bread were thrust into our hands. Tankards of beer were passed around.

'What is this?' I asked Gunari's wife. 'It is delicious, but it is not a taste I know.'

'That is hotchiwitchi.' She smiled. 'You would call it hedgehog.'

I nearly spat it out! 'But there are no spines,' I gasped, pretending I was just feeling round with my tongue.

I wonder how the Queen's cook would cope if he were asked to prepare a hedgehog!

When the feast was at an end, the men unloaded their carts. In no time at all tents had appeared all over the clearing and sleepy children were taken off to bed. I had a full belly and would like to have put my head on a pillow there and then, but Masou and I had to journey back. We took our leave of the gypsies, with plenty of messages for Rosa, and I'm afraid I do not remember much of the journey home on Elizabeth, for I nodded off against Masou's back.

Now the chapel clock is chiming eight and Mary Shelton is stirring. I can just see her curling papers bobbing above her bedclothes. Have I recorded everything important? I hope so, for I must be away to breakfast soon. Thank goodness food is not far off. I am famished, even after the hedgehog last night. One more thing: when we arrived at the palace, we sneaked in through a secret way Masou showed me – I swear he knows every inch of Whitehall – but when I turned to ask him what he would be doing this morning, he had slipped away. In faith he is becoming a mystery in himself. But no matter. That mystery will have to wait. I must concentrate my thoughts on Adam the Apothecary now, not Masou!

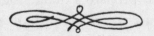

That afternoon, after dinner

I am in the chapel and intend to write as fast as my quill will let me. I cannot believe all that has happened this morning, and indeed, if someone else were to read this account, I am sure they would think me a liar.

The Spaniards left after breakfast. That was a meal best forgotten with its long tedious speeches. I have never been so uncomfortable, for I had trouble staying awake after my busy night. I had to pinch my arms several times to stop myself plummeting into my bread and beef! The Queen, of course, gave an excellent speech, but even that had my eyelids drooping. And the Spaniards seemed to have no idea what a special honour it was to have the Queen breaking her fast with them for a second time. She rarely graces us with her presence at this time of the day.

Farewells were made in the Courtyard. I note here that other ladies of the Court were being very cordial in their goodbyes, and I wondered if it was out of relief that these exotic beauties were leaving the sight and minds of the English gentlemen.

We then made our way to the Queen's Presence Chamber to await her will. She had a line of ministers who wished to speak with her and was listening to each one in turn when a servant came up to her.

'If it please Your Gracious Majesty,' he said, bowing low, 'I am sent to tell you that the apothecary has arrived.'

'Show him in,' ordered the Queen.

'What is this?' I asked Mary Shelton.

'Did you not hear at breakfast?' asked Mary. 'Her Majesty has sent for a local apothecary to help Sarah. Mrs Bea and Dr Cavendish have greatly eased Sarah's pain, but the Queen still seeks something to prevent her burns from scarring. Of course if Doctor Dee were at Court, she would turn to him, but he is away and 'tis said that this man comes highly recommended by the good Doctor Dee. Besides, he claims to have a new wonder salve that will heal Sarah's wounds.'

It must have been mentioned when I was nodding off into my beef.

I felt hope swell in my breast. I find Doctor Dee a rather frightening figure, and would always rather have my uncle to tend me when I am sick, but there is no doubt that Doctor Dee is a clever man of science and I was certain that a colleague of his would be of similar ilk.

So I thought I would cry out in shock when the apothecary was shown into the Presence Chamber, for it was none other than that charlatan, Adam! I watched him in silent fury as he took his place at the end of the line of ministers. This man was more likely to give Sarah a beard than cure her burns.

But then I went cold all over. If Adam was claiming to have a 'wonder salve', then I had been right in thinking him a strong suspect for the fire. Perhaps it was Rosa's salve that he was using.

My thoughts came tumbling over each other so fast, I could hardly keep track. How could this man be a rogue if Doctor Dee spoke so well of him? But then I reasoned that Adam probably did not know Doctor Dee at all. The slimy toad probably heard that the esteemed doctor was away from Court and then pretended an acquaintance that no one could check!

Fie, Adam! I said to myself. You have reckoned without me and my suspicions, and have done me a service by coming to Court, for as long as you are here, I can investigate you.

I knew I should warn the Queen, but then I hesitated. I had no way of *proving* that Adam had started the fire in Rosa's tent and stolen her precious haoma herb. I couldn't even tell the Queen of my suspicions without involving Rosa, and I had promised the old lady that I would keep her presence at the palace a secret. I decided that I would simply suggest to the Queen that Adam might be a charlatan and thus must be closely watched.

Adam waited for his audience, smugly surveying us all. I slipped over to Her Majesty. I had to wait while she signed some letters, but then I put myself in front of her before the next applicant could step forward. I curtsied deeply.

'You seem determined to have speech with me, Lady Grace,' the Queen said, amused.

'If it please, Your Majesty,' I answered quickly. 'I have something of great import to tell you.'

'Import, you say?' murmured the Queen. 'So

much so that I must ask these gentlemen to let you speak out of turn?'

'It concerns Lady Sarah,' I told her.

'Then walk with me to the window and back,' the Queen commanded, rising to her feet. 'You have that time to impart your "something of great import".' She turned to the waiting ministers. 'Gentlemen, I beg you give me leave to stretch my legs for a few moments.'

Of course they would do nothing else!

We made our way towards the far wall. 'It is that apothecary, Adam, Your Majesty,' I said, keeping my voice low. 'He is nothing but a fraud. I saw him at St Bartholomew's Fair. He sold my tiring woman a remedy that made her ill instead of effecting any cure. Would it not be terrible for Lady Sarah to be given false hope?'

'Indeed it would,' said the Queen. 'But I do not think you need fear. Your information does not accord with what I have been told. I have it from Mrs Champernowne that Adam has invented a miracle salve. He first used it last week at a market in Camberwell on a man badly burned. The mark was gone by nightfall, it is said. I do not believe that, but for such a tale to be spread, it does seem likely that his salve did much to reduce the burn.'

I had not expected this! It seemed that Adam had already got some sort of salve when we saw him at St Bartholomew's Fair, in which case he would have had no need to steal Rosa's haoma. But he was still a villain, I felt sure, and if the salve was not Rosa's remedy, then he had likely made it up himself – and I very much doubted he had the proper skill for such work. Sarah could be in danger of suffering more harm, just as Ellie had been.

We had reached the window. The Queen looked thoughtful, then took my hand. 'I am desperate to find some solution for poor Sarah before her burns turn to scars. Surely anything is worth a try. However, you have never led me wrong in the past so I will take your words seriously and find a compromise. I will allow this Adam to help Lady Sarah, but every move he makes will be watched. And if he plans any mischief, he will be out of here and tossed in the Thames before you can say "miscreant"!'

I sank into a curtsy and the Queen returned to her seat to deal with her ministers. It was not long before Adam was brought before her. He bowed deeply.

'You are Adam, known as an apothecary in the City?' said the Queen.

'I am only your humble servant, Your Majesty,' said the odious man smoothly, 'and if I could die now, I would be received in Heaven as the most blessed of men, for in seeing you, I have seen the Sun.'

This was clever of him, for Her Majesty loves nothing better than compliments.

'You have great words, Adam,' the Queen told him. 'And I have a great task for you. You will know of the tragic fire at Smith Field in which a woman lost her life and my Maid was injured?'

Adam looked grave. 'Indeed, My Liege. It was a great tragedy.'

'Lady Sarah Bartelmy has suffered burns, especially to her face,' the Queen went on. 'I have been told that you have a remedy for this. She is very important to me and I will reward most generously any who help her suffering.'

'Then I am blessed indeed that I can be of service to you,' said Adam. Faith! If this man simpered any more, he would melt into a puddle! 'My salve, with ingredients known only to myself, has proved most successful with burns. Your Maid is in safe hands, o Gracious Sovereign.' He turned his head as if to invite congratulations from the rest of the Court.

I was very glad that I had managed to warn the

Queen of this apothecary and his silver words and flattery.

'Mrs Champernowne will take you to Lady Sarah,' said Her Majesty. 'She will of course stay with my poor Maid and supervise the application of your wonderful cure.'

Adam made so many deep bows as he left that I thought his nose would sweep the floor.

I wasted no time and went to the Queen, pushing in before the next applicant. In fact, I believe I trod on his toe!

'May I also go with Mrs Champernowne?' I asked, ignoring the stifled groan behind me. 'I could hold Lady Sarah's hand and I would like to observe the work of the apothecary.'

I saw amusement in Her Majesty's eyes. She knew just what I meant. 'I am sure that my Mistress of the Maids will keep a very close watch on Adam,' she said. 'But you will lighten poor Sarah's mood so make haste.'

I did!

Just as I was leaving the Privy Chamber, I heard Lady Jane speaking to Lucy. 'I must consult with this Adam,' she told her, 'if he is as good as he says.'

Oh dear. Was the horrible Adam going to become very popular at Court? I soon found someone who did not think so. As I hurried along the passageway, I came across Ellie. She wore a face of thunder.

'You'll never believe who I just saw!' She spat. 'It was that fraudster, Adam. If he hadn't been with Mrs Champernowne, I would have stabbed him with . . .' She looked at the stockings she was carrying. 'I mean, I would have strangled him with these till he cried for mercy!'

'But if he was being strangled he would not have had the breath to cry for mercy,' I said, teasing her. 'Anyhow, Adam is here on the Queen's orders. She wants him to try out a new salve on Lady Sarah's burns.'

'Don't let him near her, Grace,' said Ellie, looking horrified. 'He'll have her looking like a wolf or worse.'

'Be sure I will not let anything of the sort happen to Lady Sarah,' I told her. 'And it may suit our purpose to have Adam here at the palace, for we can watch him like hawks.'

Ellie would have argued more but I had no time to linger. I caught up with my quarries as they crossed the Privy Garden. I was quite out of breath with my dash. Adam swept me a bow, but I think Mrs Champernowne was a little displeased with my unladylike arrival.

'I was sent by the Queen,' I panted. 'To distract Lady Sarah.'

Mrs Champernowne looked as if she wanted to berate me for running like a boy, but then she smiled. 'I believe you could distract the devil himself, dear Lady Grace,' she said. And as we reached the stairway to climb up to Sarah's chamber, she took my hand and squeezed it. 'If you can't bring a smile to my lady's face then I don't know who can.'

When we entered Lady Sarah's room, I saw that it was full of flowers and trinkets. And there were plates of sweetmeats too, but they lay untouched. I knew who had brought all these things – Daniel Cheshire. But his generous gifts had had no effect on poor Sarah. She lay back on her pillow, gazing at nothing. Her face was very pale except for the livid red burn on her left cheek. I found myself fearing that such a mark was surely permanent and would spoil her beauty. Then I saw the looking glass in her limp hand and I felt heartsick for her. She must have been seeing the dreadful evidence for herself.

Mrs Champernowne was bustling about fetching a basin and a cloth. 'Now, Lady Sarah,' she said. 'Here is Adam the Apothecary sent direct by

Her Majesty to help you. He has a wondrous salve for that poor face.'

Sarah sighed deeply. 'Nothing can help me,' she whispered.

'Have faith, my lady,' said Adam in his oily voice. 'You will be amazed at what my potion can do.'

Sarah turned her head away.

A moment later

Great heavens! Carmina has just flown past the chapel door, shrieking that she has seen a hobbling duck – such an ill omen. Well, it is for the duck, I suppose.

Anyway, Mr Silver Tongue seemed lost for words at Sarah's utter lack of interest in his wondrous salve. Then he rallied. 'Now, Mrs Champernowne, you must have that cloth ready.'

Mrs Champernowne bridled at his peremptory tone but she said nothing. It seemed to me that Master Apothecary was getting too big for his boots.

I sat on the chair next to the bed. Taking Sarah's hand, I gently prised away the looking glass. She did not stop me.

'How pretty your chamber is looking,' I said in a hearty voice. 'Is this all the work of Mr Cheshire? He is a devoted suitor to be sure.'

Sarah sighed. 'He is a kind man and that is all this is — kindness. He will not want to be stuck with someone as ugly as I have become. He will wait a few weeks and then he will find someone else to court.'

'No,' I said. 'I do not believe it. He is proving himself true to you and to you only.'

She shook her head. 'That will pass, and I will bear him no grudge when he stops coming to see me.' She closed her eyes as if she did not want to discuss the matter any further. I kept a tight hold of her hand and got ready to watch Adam like a hawk. I was feeling very nervous for Lady Sarah.

He took the cloth from Mrs Champernowne and laid it by Sarah's other arm. 'There is a small burn here,' he said. 'I will apply some of my salve to that first. I have never seen any ill effects from my potion, but I'll not put it on a face without testing it first.'

I thanked Heaven for that! At least any ill effects would be less noticeable there.

Adam turned to Mrs Champernowne. 'Assist my lady to put her arm on the cloth.'

'Humph!' Mrs Champernowne muttered,

looking as if she would like to remind Adam that he was a mere apothecary and should not order her about like a servant, but she held her tongue.

Adam made a great show of inspecting the burn on Sarah's arm. Then, reaching into a small bag tied to his belt, he produced a small black jar. He pulled out the stopper and, taking a small piece of flat bone, scooped up a pea-sized amount of his ointment. It was the colour of porridge and thicker than cream. Using the bone he smeared it over the raw burned skin, making Sarah wince. Convinced as I was that this man was a fraud, I waited for him to make some bold statement about his instant cure, but he did not. He merely replaced the stopper in the jar.

I looked closely at the burn. 'Nothing is happening,' I said.

'The salve needs time to work,' Adam told me. 'I will review the matter in a few hours.' And he swept from the room as if he were the King.

There followed a tedious morning. Her Majesty was in private conversation with Secretary Cecil and Mr Walsingham, no doubt in relation to the search of our Spanish visitors' luggage. This left the rest of us to our own devices. I determined to fetch my daybooke and make an entry. I had much to write. However, I had just made it to the staircase when I heard Mrs Champernowne's voice echoing down the passageways.

'What is amiss?' asked Mary Shelton, putting aside her book of prayers.

'Mrs Champernowne is calling for us to go to Lady Sarah,' said Carmina. 'I fear to go. Has poor Sarah had a relapse?'

I got up, wishing to waste no time, and my fellow Maids followed me as we ran to Sarah's chamber, forgetting all decorum. We passed a page running in the opposite direction in search of the Queen. My heart was in my mouth. What would we find?

We burst into the bedchamber and stopped short. What a wonderful sight greeted us. Lady Sarah was sitting up in bed and there was a small smile on her lips. She held out her arm to us.

'Look!' she whispered.

The redness of the burn had faded a little and it did not seem as rough.

'It hurts much less,' said Sarah, with a note of wonder in her voice.

I smiled and laughed with the rest, but I confess I was extremely puzzled. I had been so convinced that Adam was a trickster, and yet here was his salve doing exactly as he had promised. I saw him standing in the corner of the room. He looked the picture of a grave, pious healer. Was he just that? Had I made a mistake?

At this moment the Queen arrived, closely followed by Daniel Cheshire. Once the curtsies and bows were out of the way, he took himself to Lady Sarah's side and held her hand tightly. I quickly looked at the Queen for signs of displeasure at this young man's devotion towards her precious Maid of Honour, but there were none.

'Look at my arm, Your Majesty,' said Lady Sarah, with more life in her voice than I had heard for a while. 'Look at my arm, Daniel.' She turned to the apothecary. 'Oh, please, Master Adam, put some on my face that I may regain my beauty.'

'Sarah, be patient,' urged Mr Cheshire. 'Do not rest all your hopes in this salve. It may not work as well on your face – not that I would care.'

Sarah did not heed his words. 'Please, Master Adam,' she pleaded.

Adam stepped forward to the bed, took out his little black jar and did as she asked. With a contented sigh, Lady Sarah fell back onto the pillow.

'Mr Cheshire does right to urge caution,' said the apothecary. 'I believe my potion will work well but it will be slow. I must apply it morn and night for several days yet.'

'Then you will be my guest for that time,' said the Queen, 'and I will ensure that you are treated well in gratitude for your care of my Maid.'

Adam bent in one of his sweeping bows, from which position he addressed the Queen. 'O Gracious Majesty, I could ask for no greater honour, but may I beg a humble boon?'

'What is that, my man?' asked the Queen.

'Will you allow my wife to join me here?' asked Adam.

'A small boon indeed,' said the Queen, 'and gladly granted. Now I believe Lady Sarah would do better without all you Maids gaping at her.'

We took the hint and left. I sent for Ellie and we walked among the statues of the Privy Garden. I told her about the improvement in Sarah's burns.

'Have we been hasty?' I asked her. 'Could it be that by some unhappy chance you received the wrong medicine? Perhaps the labels had become switched.'

'You may well think that, Grace,' growled Ellie, 'but what sort of healer can't label his jars right?'

I left her and went back to wait on the Queen. I did not know what to think.

However, an hour later I knew exactly what was what!

We were sitting on cushions near the Queen. She was talking quietly with Secretary Cecil – those Spaniards have given cause for much work, it seems. Mary was reading quietly to us and I had Ellie by my side as she attended to a torn wrist ruff. (What a scolding that had earned me from Mrs Champernowne, and all I had done was let Henri, the Queen's dog, get a little excited so that he tore my ruff!)

Anyhow, all was calm when the page at the door stirred and announced Adam and his wife.

And now I knew that there could be nothing honest about this apothecary, for his wife was none other than Sylvia, the fortune-teller who had told Ellie she must have the Miracle Lovage Remedy that had made her so ill! What a deception these people were practising! Sylvia, the distressed fortune-teller, tells a customer that they will be gravely ill, and lo and behold, the only apothecary who has the expensive cure required is Adam, her husband. Adam then sells the poor victim something to make the bad fortune come true! And, in their despair and pain, the unhappy victim might even return and part with more coin in hopes of being cured. How evil! Surely one who could do such a thing would not hesitate to set fire to Rosa's tent and steal her herb to make himself rich. I would have shouted his guilt to the rooftops – but still I had no proof!

I felt Ellie stiffen by my side as she saw them enter. I wondered if I would have to hold her back, but she kept her peace.

To add insult to injury, once they had been presented to the Queen, Adam and Sylvia had the gall to walk over to us and enquire after Ellie's health! I knew that Ellie would start to berate them then, so I took action for which I have apologized a thousand times since. Standing slightly in front of her to shield my actions, I elbowed Ellie in the gut. Poor Ellie doubled over as if in pain, although I did not jab her so very hard!

'She is still poorly, my brave Ellie,' I told them. 'But we see some improvement thanks to the lovage medicine.'

They smiled – most insincerely, I am sure – and moved away. I was disgusted that they should think me such a fool as to believe their lying words, but I held my disgust within, for my thoughts were racing. I was sure I had the truth of the matter at last!

'Oh, Ellie,' I said loudly. 'This wrist ruff will not do. Come quickly and fit me with another.'

With the Queen's permission, we left and hurried to my chamber.

'That Adam and his wife were in it together to poison me!' Ellie exploded as soon as the door was closed.

'Not only that,' I told her in excitement, 'but I am certain it was he who set fire to Rosa's tent, stole her haoma and is now passing *Rosa's* cure off as his own. The tale of having cured someone a week ago must be all a lie. They are nothing but a couple of rogues!'

'More than rogues,' said Ellie fiercely. 'He tried to kill that dear old lady.'

'You could be right, Ellie,' I agreed. 'But even if he wanted to kill Rosa, he cannot have known that Lady Sarah was in there too. Surely he would not have wanted to harm one of the Queen's ladies, with the severe punishment that that would bring.'

'Whatever the truth, you must go straight to the Queen and denounce him,' demanded Ellie.

'I need evidence, o hasty one,' I said. 'Mere words cannot prove him a fake and a would-be murderer. And he is now well liked at Court because of his treatment of Lady Sarah, so I must tread carefully.'

'Don't say he's going to get away with it!' Ellie cried, aghast.

'Not if I have anything to do with it,' I said grimly. 'But first, we need some of Adam's miracle

salve so that we can take it to Rosa. She will be
able to tell us for certain if it has her stolen haoma
in it or not.'

Ellie grinned. 'And then we'll 'ave him!' she
cheered.

I said nothing. I had a sneaking suspicion it
would not be that simple.

An hour later

I am sitting in Lady Sarah's bedchamber. And I
have just done the impossible. I have bored her to
sleep with her favourite subject – gossip! I have to
admit that perhaps I do not know any exciting
gossip, and mayhap the tale of Sir Pelham Poucher's
doublet was rather dull. In any case, she has escaped
from it and I have the chance to write in my
daybooke.

With the Queen's permission, I came back to
Sarah's bedchamber to keep her company. I truly
wish to keep Sarah in good cheer, but I also hoped
I would find the salve here. How easy that would
have made things, but of course there was no
sign of it.

'Adam took it away with him,' Sarah told me when I asked. 'He must safeguard his secret and ensure it does not fall into another's hands. Just think what a tricky rogue could do with it.'

I wanted to say, 'Heal people,' but I held my tongue. I had been foolish to think Adam would let the salve out of his sight. He was a cheat and would expect others to behave as he did. Also he must fear discovery.

'He will be back soon,' said Lady Sarah, touching the burn on her face with her fingertips. 'I am to have a second application. Oh, Grace, is this not a wonder cure?'

Already the mark seemed fainter.

I smiled at her. 'It certainly seems to be helping,' I said. 'Now let me acquaint you with the latest goings-on at Court, for you are missing it all being up here.'

Poor Lady Sarah. If I am able to prove that Adam is a villain, then she will find that the man who is saving her looks is the man who almost killed her in the first place! I am determined to get some of that salve and show that it contains Rosa's secret haoma. I hope that will suffice in exposing Adam and his wife. I am not sure what else I can—

Hell's teeth! It went very dark in here for a

moment, but it was merely a cloud across the sun. If Carmina had been here, doubtless she would have been full of dire pronouncements about the light in our lives going out.

That evening, before bed

It is near to midnight and I should be asleep like Mary Shelton, but I feel excitement bubbling inside me which will make it hard to put my head on the pillow. I am sure that with the morrow the mystery will be at an end, for I have a plan. Of course, if I went to sleep, then the morning would come all the quicker, but I must first finish my account of the day.

Earlier, in Sarah's chamber, I had to put down my daybooke in rather a hurry, for Adam the Apothecary swaggered in, with Mrs Champernowne and a page bustling at his heels. The last person I would want to read my private thoughts is that fraudulent man (though I would not wish Mrs C to read my words either!).

I was very pleased to see that Adam was taken aback to find me there. However, he quickly recovered his charm – if a snake can be said to have charm.

'Lady Grace,' he said, bowing low. Faith! The man bows more than a lackey. 'You are a devoted nurse, to be sure.'

I noticed that the black jar was no longer tied to his belt, but now had pride of place on a silver tray, carried by the young servant. Adam beckoned him into the middle of the room and bade him stand there. Then he took a small dish of oil with a wick and placed it by Lady Sarah's bed. He lit the wick and a foul smell permeated the room.

'What? Where?' Poor Sarah was wrenched from her sleep. 'Faugh! What is that stench?' she cried.

'An unguent of my own design, my lady,' said Adam, 'to promote a harmonious balance in the place of healing.'

Sarah covered her nose with a kerchief. 'Can I not have the geranium oil? I liked that.'

Adam shook his head. 'I do not know who suggested you have that stuff in here,' he said, 'but it is most dangerous. Anyone who understands these things would know that geranium oil is home to tiny demons who carry sickness on their wings. You would never recover, breathing in such tainted air.'

By Old Father Thames, the man speaks as much rubbish as is found on the palace compost heap! I wished that Mrs Bea and Rosa were there to hear it. Even Mrs Champernowne looked confused, but she held her tongue.

Adam turned to the tray held by the page and took up the small piece of bone he had used earlier. I had to find a way to get some of the salve. I realized that his back would be turned while he applied it to Lady Sarah's face, so I would have a few minutes as long as I distracted the boy as well. But how could I actually get some of the ointment? I was thinking furiously.

Adam was now making his way to the bed. He began to apply the salve gently to Sarah's cheek. I edged nearer to the page. I planned to point out something through the window and then while the young boy's head was turned I would hook my finger into the black pot. But how could I keep the sample in such a way? I looked desperately round the room for something I could put it in.

'What ails you, Grace?' asked Mrs Champernowne. 'Why do you fidget so?'

I had forgotten for the moment that she was in the room; she had been so quiet. Now I had two people to distract, for she would never tolerate me fiddling with the precious salve.

'Oh, nothing,' I said airily. 'I am just a trifle stiff from sitting for so long.'

 149

I was glad I had given her this simple answer. Mrs Champernowne is one of the most superstitious at Court and would put my jiggling down to ill fortune if she could. I had seen she was wearing a brooch made from a wishbone for luck.

I walked near to the page. Perhaps I could admire the carving of the silver tray and, in doing so, 'accidentally' trail my sleeve in the potion. Rosa and Mrs Bea could then scrape it off and make their analysis. Perfect. I walked over and inspected the embossed deer on the tray for ages, but somehow I had difficulty getting my sleeve in the right place.

'Is there ought amiss with your arm, Lady Grace?' asked Adam. The rogue had turned and was staring at me. 'Mayhap I should take a look at it when I have finished here.'

'No, no,' I said hurriedly. 'I was just chasing away a fly.' Then I had an idea. While I tried to think of another way to get some of the salve, I would engage the apothecary in conversation and hope he would betray himself with his words in front of Mrs Champernowne and Lady Sarah.

'I expect you did a good trade at the St Bartholomew's Fair, Master Adam,' I said sweetly.

'My aim is always to heal,' he said in a pious tone.

'The poor lady who died in the fire was a famous healer,' I carried on. 'Rosa, I believe her name was. It is so terrible that all her gifts are lost to us now. What a dreadful fate!'

Adam's expression did not change at the mention of her name. I moved to the other side of the tray. I had decided to trip, knock into the page and make sure he tipped everything onto the floor. Then I would help to pick it all up and by happy chance, my finger would dig into the ointment. It was worth risking a chiding for clumsiness from Mrs Champernowne.

'The loss of any life in a fire is a horror,' said Adam, reaching out to smooth a little of the cream paste onto Sarah's neck. 'What fortune you had, my lady, to be rescued from the flames.' He turned to me. 'Let us not talk of it any more in front of Lady Sarah, for she will be wanting to forget her ordeal, and indeed her healing will be much helped if she can.'

The villain! He was daring to chastize me – and with such a smug smile on his face. Well, he would not be so smug when I had got some of his salve and showed him for the fraud he was. I had decided that bumping into the page might not be enough to spill the tray. I would have to fall, lean very heavily on one end and thus catapult the black jar into the air. Then, when I retrieved it, I would get a good sample and hide it in my wrist ruff.

Adam was still talking and I had not been heeding his words until now. Suddenly they entered my consciousness.

'Of course, such folk as Rosa deserve to die in such a way. It is a just punishment for those who put curses and jinxes upon innocent folk.'

My acting skills were sorely tried by this man. I wanted to strike him but I had to act the pleasant maid. How could he speak of Rosa and the gypsies in this way? I noticed now that as Adam spoke, he fiddled with a pendant hanging round his neck. It was a pentangle.

'A five-pointed star,' I said, pointing to it. 'That is an unusual design.'

'I wear it as protection,' he said. 'You can never be too careful, not with such evil people about.'

'Are you saying Rosa and the other traders were gypsies?' I asked, putting a shocked expression on my face. 'But surely, if that is so, you should have told the authorities. You could be in trouble for hiding that.'

'Oh, no,' Adam said hastily, 'I'm not saying that. Rosa and her kind are just pedlars who foolishly dabble in the black arts and thus deserve all they get.' He leaned back, admiring his work. Fie! He had finished and I had no sample of the salve. I had to do my catapult trick now.

'Grace!' It was Mrs Champernowne. 'You have disturbed Master Adam for long enough. Come away with you.'

The look on her face brooked no argument. I had little choice but to leave empty-handed.

I decided that I needed the help of my two friends, so I set off in search of Masou, collecting Ellie on the way. That part was easy – Ellie had told me she would be gathering lavender to lay under my pillow for sweet dreams; however, finding Masou was another matter. I assumed he would be practising with Mr Somers's troupe and, as it was a fine day, I thought they would be outside. But there was no sign of them on the Bowling Green or in the Privy Garden. Ellie and I walked across the grounds and at last came upon Masou in the Tilting Yard. He was flapping an old sheet about, but as soon as he saw us, he bundled it up and threw it to the ground.

'Fair ladies.' He gave a small bow and I knew he was being careful in case anyone was watching us and would see us talking as friends. There was a stand of seats from when the Queen had last watched some horsemanship, so I pointed to it and we made our separate ways behind the seats, where we would be hidden from view.

'What were you up to with that sheet?' I asked.

'All will be revealed in the fullness of time,' he said, and would say no more although I threatened to tweak his nose!

'Mayhap you are too busy to help me with my mystery,' I said, hoping the words would tempt him to help in my quest against Adam.

It worked!

'I am ever at your service, fair Grace,' he said. 'There are things that only one as skilled as I can do.'

He is right, of course, but I would not tell him that or his head will swell.

'I need to get into Adam's chambers,' I said. 'I want some of the special salve he is using on Lady Sarah, but he and his wife must be out of the way so that I am not discovered.'

'A diversion.' Masou beamed. 'My favourite task. Leave it with me, dear ladies. I will be but a moment.'

He skipped off.

'What's he going to do?' wondered Ellie.

'I have no idea,' I replied.

We began to make our way back across the

Tilting Yard when suddenly we saw Masou again – this time with Adam in tow. We hid behind a tree to avoid being seen. I wondered where Sylvia was. We did not have to wait long to find out.

'I'm sorry your good wife was not in your chamber,' said Masou in the voice he uses for masques. He has a clever knack of projecting it without shouting. He was doing it now so that Ellie and I would hear. 'I would like to have met her,' he went on, and I knew Masou was telling us that the coast was clear. 'Now, my problem is this terrible limp, Master Apothecary,' he went on. 'I cannot show you inside for I need room for my demonstration.'

'I see no limp when you walk,' said Adam, puzzled.

'Oh, I have no issue with walking,' said Masou. 'Look!' And he strutted around the grass like a peacock. 'But when I do this . . .' Masou took a short run, then somersaulted, performed a handspring and finished with a forward roll. 'By Shaitan!' he whimpered. 'My ankle does hurt now.' And he limped across the same grass in such a comical manner that it was all Ellie and I could do not to laugh out loud.

Adam looked quite perplexed. 'Is this a jest?' he asked.

Masou stopped. 'No,' he said, 'it is most serious for an acrobat like me to be so afflicted.' He jangled the coins in his purse. 'I am, of course, the Queen's favourite fool.'

'Walk again for me.' Adam was all smoothness now. 'Let me study your gait.'

I had been so entertained by Masou's performance I had forgotten its purpose for a moment, but now I nudged Ellie. 'Quick!' I whispered. 'We must away to Adam's chamber.'

But what a shock we got when we pushed open the door to his rooms. Sylvia was sitting at a table. Her errand, whatever it was, must have been done.

'Can I help you, my lady?' she said, getting to her feet and curtsying.

'Yes, indeed,' I said, squeezing Ellie's arm in the hope she would get the message that she was to play along with my words. 'My servant Ellie was so impressed with your accurate reading at the fair that she has come to hear more.' I delved into my purse, which I had on a string of beads around my waist, and produced some coins.

'What an honour.' Sylvia smiled. 'Come to the table, Ellie, and we shall see what we shall see . . .'

Adam and his wife had been given a good, well-lit set of chambers. The Queen had said he would be treated well for healing Lady Sarah and she had been true to her word. There was a table, where Sylvia was standing, and four sturdy oak chairs. Piles of books, with long medical-sounding titles, were stacked in one corner. I wondered if Adam actually read these or if they were just for show. Two smaller tables stood on either side of the fireplace, covered in red cloths. And there on one was the silver tray and the black jar containing the salve I needed.

Ellie crossed Sylvia's palm, and Sylvia took her hand and studied it hard. 'Oh, what a joyous future lies ahead!' she cried out. 'Oh, what happiness! A good man and five sturdy children – although it does depend upon you taking the Miracle Lovage Remedy for your health.'

'I was meaning to ask you about that,' said Ellie, in a quiet voice.

I stiffened. What was her plan? Was she going to confront Sylvia about the dreadful potion?

'You see, I want to buy some more.' Ellie continued, shooting me a look that clearly said *Hold your tongue, Grace!*

Sylvia leaped to her feet. 'Of course, of course,' she trilled. 'I will fetch it immediately. My husband keeps it in his supply satchel.'

She went off into their bedchamber and I

realized Ellie's ploy: she was giving me the chance to procure some of the healing salve. I darted over and pulled the stopper from the jar. There was no time for delicacy, so I stuck my finger in and pulled it out, covered in the thick creamy salve. Ellie saw what I was about and came and replaced the stopper for me, while I bent my finger inside my fist and clasped my other hand around it as if in prayer to hide the cream.

I was just moving across to sit down while we waited for Sylvia to return when something about the books caught my eye. The spine of the bottom one looked odd. I forgot about sitting down and went to have a closer look. I soon saw that this was no book, but a metal box – and I thought I knew which one.

'Ellie!' I hissed. 'Quick!'

She scuttled over to me and I went to point, nearly losing all the salve on my finger. I quickly shut my hand again.

'It's Rosa's box,' I whispered. 'Can you get it?'

'I will be with you very soon, my ladies,' came Sylvia's voice. 'I have to find a suitable bottle for the remedy.'

Ellie grasped the box and pulled at it. The stack of books swayed and I thought they would tumble but she righted them just in time. Then she stood up triumphantly, showing me the rose etched in the lid of the box.

'Now we've got 'im!' she grinned.

There was a noise in the other chamber, and Ellie swiftly tucked the box under her skirts as Sylvia reappeared, clutching a small bottle. But now Ellie had to double up in order to walk while keeping the box hidden.

'Just in time,' she groaned to Sylvia. 'See how the pain takes me.'

Clever Ellie, I thought. And I made for the door.

Sylvia gave a small cough. I turned and inwardly cursed my foolishness. Sylvia wanted payment for the potion, of course, but I could not reach inside my purse without revealing the salve on my finger. I did the only thing I could think of . . .

'Stop fussing, girl,' I said sharply to Ellie, 'and come here. This kind woman is waiting for her honest payment and you are thinking only of yourself. Now, take the money from my purse and give it to her.'

I stood with my hands clasped before me and stared into the distance while poor Ellie clutching her belly — and the box — found the coins.

Once at a safe distance, we gave way to whoops of laughter. Then we took ourselves to Mrs Bea. Ellie had now managed to wrap the box in her

apron and she clutched the lovage remedy in her
other hand. I was just wondering why she had
insisted on buying more when she spoke.

'You must be proud of me, Grace, for I wanted
to pull that harpy's hair and stamp on her toes for
what she and her husband did to my poor insides.'

'I am very glad you showed such restraint,' I told
her. 'We have everything we went for.'

'Oh, I have much more than that,' said Ellie
mysteriously. 'Mr and Mrs Adam will soon wish
they hadn't meddled with me!'

We were delighted to find Rosa sitting at a table
and looking much better. I held out my sticky
finger and she examined the salve. First she sniffed
it, then she tasted a bit on the tip of her tongue –
just as she had done when testing the so-called
Miracle Lovage Remedy.

'Yes' – she nodded – 'that has been made with
haoma resin to my recipe. But how do we prove
that Adam stole it?'

'Like this!' cried Ellie and, with a flourish
worthy of Masou, she unwrapped her apron and
produced the metal box with its rose etched on the
lid.

Rosa gasped in delight, took it gratefully and
opened it. Inside, wrapped in linen, was a brown,

grainy paste. It put me in mind of ground mustard seeds.

'Here is my precious supply,' she sighed, and there were tears in her eyes. She pointed to some etching on the inside of the lid. I recognized pictures of a broken egg and a honeycomb. 'And this is how he knew the recipe.'

'Yet is this enough evidence to lay before the Queen?' I asked. 'She is pleased with Adam for the change in Sarah's burns and will not accuse him willingly. I think she will believe me when I say that the salve and the box were found in his room, but what is to stop him saying he bought the box and had no idea it was Rosa's?'

Mrs Bea nodded. 'We need a confession.'

We sat glumly for a few moments.

'I am sorry, Rosa,' I said, getting to my feet, 'but I fear we must return the box to Adam's chamber before he discovers it has gone. He will be on his guard and may, indeed, make his escape if he knows we suspect him. But I will think of some way to trap him, and very soon, so that you may have it back.'

She gave me the box. 'I trust you, Lady Grace,' she said simply.

'Now, how to put it back . . .' I wondered.

'Leave that to me, my lady,' said Ellie. 'I will take

Sylvia a small thank-you gift for my lovely lovage and I'll stick it back just as we found it.' She had a funny smile on her face.

'What mischief are you planning for Adam and his wife?' I asked.

'Nothing you need worry about,' she replied enigmatically.

All in all it has been a very strange day. I have found the proof I need but, alas, I have had to put it back. I am determined that Adam is not going to get away with his heinous crime, but how am I going to get him to confess – and in front of the Queen?

Wait! I have just remembered how he fiddled with the pendant around his neck and how his stall at Smith Field was covered in charms to ward off evil. This devious apothecary seems most superstitious. Perhaps that can be used to my advantage . . .

The Twenty‑seventh Day of August, in the Year of Our Lord 1570

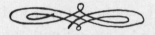

After dinner

God-a-mercy! At last I have a place to write
where I shall not be disturbed. First I tried the
window by my chamber, but no sooner was my
bum on the ledge than Mrs Champernowne
shooed me off, telling me I looked untidy. Then I
found a seat in a kitchen storeroom, but a servant
came in and nearly dropped the dish he was
carrying. I suppose he did not expect to see a
Maid of Honour among the platters. So now I am
in the Buttery, right behind a cider press. Surely I
am safe here!

I must be brief – we are attending the Queen
soon – but I have thought up a scheme that may
solve this mystery once and for all. This is how it
came about.

This morning, after breakfast, Adam and Sylvia
were to have an audience with the Queen. We all

waited in the Presence Chamber, and everyone was chatting about the charming apothecary who could work miracles on Lady Sarah's face. Well, to tell the truth it was mostly the women who were excited about the evil-eyed ratsbane! (I heard a ferry passenger who ran off without paying his fare being called this by one of the watermen, and have wanted to use it ever since!)

'I have a blemish under my eye,' said Lucy, who sat on a cushion next to me. 'Think you he will have something to make it go?'

I peered hard at her. There was the tiniest mark just below her lashes. No one could possibly have noticed if she had not pointed it out!

'I am certain he could,' breathed Carmina. 'And I will pay him anything to make my nails stronger. See how they crack – well, they do in the winter, anyway.'

'I cannot find anything to make my moustaches curl successfully,' piped up Sir Edmund Renfrew.

I turned away to hide my chuckles and looked towards the door. Adam and his wife were late – unheard of when the Queen commands. Her Majesty's lips were pursed tighter and tighter. Finally she rose with an angry rustle of jewellery and skirts.

'I see that our guests consider themselves too

important to grace us with their presence,' she said crisply. 'I shall wait no more. There are matters of State to which I must attend.'

We were dismissed, and the Queen swept off to her Privy Chamber. I felt sorry for her ministers as her mood would not be sweet.

I caught up with Ellie at the top of the stairs. An awful idea had occurred to me. 'Do you think Adam and his wife could have got wind of my suspicions and run away?' I asked.

'I'll bet you all the Queen's gold they haven't,' said Ellie, grinning.

'How can you be so sure?' I demanded.

'You'll see,' was all the annoying girl would say.

We walked in silence. I was wrapped up in my worries that my prey had escaped – for how could Ellie be sure that was not the case?

Then Ellie cleared her throat loudly and nodded towards the passage ahead. To my relief, there was Adam. He looked awful. He was white as a sheet and staggered towards us, clutching his belly with one hand and his pentangle pendant with the other. When he saw us, he tried to make a polite bow, which turned into a groan.

'My lady,' he said, and I only just caught the words, he was stooped so low. 'I fear I have done a terrible thing. I am so ill that I could not attend

Her Majesty, and could not even send word, for my wife has been likewise smitten.'

'How unfortunate,' I said, thinking that surely this was not just playacting and white lead.

'I hope the Queen will forgive me,' he said pitifully. 'I am on my way to make my apologies in person.'

I tried not to enjoy the picture in my mind of him moaning and groaning outside the Queen's chambers, waiting for an audience.

'What is it that ails you?' I asked, trying to sound sympathetic.

Adam straightened a little and showed us the pendant clutched in his sweating hand. 'There's an evil eye trying to lay low my body,' he croaked. 'I must fight it with this.' He waved the pendant around in the air as if the evil eye might pop out of a doorway at any minute. Then he suddenly turned green. 'Forgive me, I must go.' He stumbled away and we soon heard the splattering of puke on the floor.

'What a shame!' said Ellie, with obvious delight. 'He don't look too good.'

I stared at her closely. 'Ellie, did you have anything to do with this?'

'Course not, Grace,' she chuckled. 'A little drop of his Miracle Lovage Remedy *might* have got itself into those sweetmeats I took to him and Sylvia yesterday – but accidents will happen.'

'How careless of you, Ellie,' I said, pretending to be cross. But I caught a naughty gleam in her eye and we both collapsed in giggles.

Courtiers going by looked at us askance, we were cackling so loudly. (They soon stopped in their tracks and forgot all about us when the smell of puke hit them further down the passage, though!)

'Best bit about it,' gasped Ellie when we had recovered enough to talk, 'is that Adam has no idea why he's ill. His head's full of it being evil spirits!'

'He is indeed most superstitious if his mind always turns straight to the supernatural when he is ill.' Then it came to me – the ghost of an idea. 'This might perchance be the key to Adam's downfall!' I gave Ellie a hug. 'Thank you, dear friend,' I said in excitement. 'You have helped me think of a plan which will unravel this mystery – a trap to catch a couple of rats.'

'I don't know what you're talking about, Grace,' said Ellie, scratching her head.

'And I have no time to tell you,' I said. 'I must catch up with Adam.'

I darted off down the corridor, following the smell. Adam had not gone far. He was round the corner, leaning against a wall. I kept as much distance as I could between us, but I had to speak to him, for he was going to give me an excuse to seek a very important audience with Her Majesty.

'You are so ill,' I said. My voice sounded rather strangled. Well, it is hard to speak when you are trying not to breath through your nose. 'Please allow me to give your excuses to the Queen.'

Adam looked doubtful. 'You are kindness itself, my lady,' he said, and he seemed so pathetically grateful that I had to remind myself what a nasty man he really is. 'But if Her Majesty sees me with her own eyes, she will know that I speak true.'

He had a point. Now what could I say? Fortunately inspiration struck. 'But what if she smells you with her own nose also?' I said earnestly.

Adam's brow furrowed. 'I hadn't thought of that,' he said sorrowfully. 'Then I accept your offer, and please say I will attend the Queen the minute I am able. I am most concerned that she should know only the severest illness keeps me from attending her.'

You are most concerned about getting your hands on the Queen's money and a place at Court, I thought, but I curtsied solemnly.

I left him as quickly as I could, and not just because of the smell. I had what I was after – an excuse to disturb the Queen and take her from her State papers.

Her Majesty burst out of her Privy Chamber, wrenching the doors from the guards' hands. She was still in a foul temper, for she gave an oath that I will not repeat here for fear my daybooke starts to sizzle!

I fell into a deep curtsy.

'I hope you will make this interruption worth my while, my lady,' stormed the Queen. 'I have wasted enough of the morning as it is.'

'Indeed, Your Majesty,' I said. 'I bring news of Adam the Apothecary.'

'News?' the Queen bellowed. 'No doubt you are come to tell me that he slept too late, or that he found something better to do than attend his monarch.'

Servants and courtiers were backing off. Things sometimes take to the air when the Queen is displeased. And I was right under her nose. A dangerous place to be!

'For God's sake get up, Grace!' snapped the Queen. 'And stop cringing before me. Anyone would think I was an ogre!'

'How so, My Liege? Even the greatest ogre would quail before you . . . ' I dared to say, before I could stop myself. Her eyes flashed dangerously. 'For your magnificence would dazzle him,' I finished breathlessly.

Luckily the Queen burst into a great guffaw of laughter and all around her breathed again. She does blow hot and cold!

'Thank you, Goddaughter,' she said, patting my hand. 'You have taken me from my worries. Now, say, what of this Adam – damn him for insulting me.'

'I have much to tell,' I said in a low voice. 'But it must be told away from the ears of the Court.'

As soon as we were in a private chamber, Her Majesty bade me sit and impart my news. Her eyes grew hard and steely as my tale unfolded.

'I can scarcely credit it!' she burst out when I was done. 'This apothecary who is effecting so wonderful a cure on poor Lady Sarah is the one who caused her burns in the first place?'

'I believe so,' I said. 'Everything he has done is for his own ends. He means to be rich and famous with the stolen haoma resin – and he does not care who he hurts in the process. His wife is little better.'

'Then they must be brought to justice. I will not have anyone do harm to one of my precious Maids of Honour.' The Queen gently touched my cheek.

'Let me think,' she went on. 'What proof have we? We cannot prove Adam has the box unlawfully.' She looked sharply at me. 'I warrant my Lady Pursuivant has hatched a clever plan to catch the miscreants. I can see eagerness in your eyes, Grace. Out with it!'

I nodded. My plan needed the Queen's full approval, for she would play a part in my trap. I was worried she would not give me leave to act upon it.

'Adam and his wife believe that they have killed Rosa, the old woman whose tent they burned,' I began.

'And they show no remorse!' put in Her Majesty bitterly.

'They are heartless,' I agreed. 'Yet I find them to be most superstitious people, and think we can work on this weakness. Adam already believes demons are after him and causing his sickness. I wonder if he believes he is being punished for Rosa's death. If we can contrive to make Rosa appear before Adam and his wife as a ghost, I think it will be enough to make them confess their crimes.'

The Queen looked interested, so I went on enthusiastically. 'It should be a simple matter to set up. Rosa is here at Whitehall so there will be no difficulty in—' My hand flew to my mouth. I had been so caught up in my plan that I had forgotten my promise to Rosa and Mrs Bea. No one was to know of Rosa's whereabouts. What would happen now?

But to my surprise the Queen merely smiled. 'I would be a poor monarch indeed if I did not know what goes on in my own palace,' she said simply. 'Mrs Bea's patient will suffer no disturbance from me.'

I felt a little silly. Also, I was thinking that she does not know *everything* that goes on, and blushed. But truly she is most extraordinary – and very good at turning a blind eye when she needs to.

'So if Your Majesty pleases, you will summon Adam and his wife to the audience they missed,' I said. 'Then Rosa will appear, but everyone must pretend that they do not see her so that Adam and his wife will be convinced that she is a spirit from the grave that only they – as her murderers – can see.'

'This will take some fine acting from us all,' mused the Queen. 'And what do you expect to happen after that?'

'The confession, I hope,' I said. 'I believe that the sight of the ghost of their victim should bring them gibbering to their knees and begging forgiveness for her death.'

'Your instincts are always good, Grace,' said the

Queen, 'yet I counsel you to think on this carefully. If you are wrong in this matter, it will bring disgrace and dishonour to my Court. I will not be known as a ruler who plays cruel jests upon her subjects. Are you sure we should pursue this course of action?'

I did not hesitate a second. 'Yes, I am,' I said.

The Queen nodded. 'Then I will have them bought before me this very afternoon.'

At eleven of the clock a message came from Adam saying that he and Sylvia were well enough be able to attend the noontide meal. This gave me plenty of time to plant the seed about the curse, before their audience with the Queen. I sent Ellie off, as she had a mission of her own, but not before I cautioned her.

'Promise me you have not given the wicked pair another dose of their medicine,' I said. 'My plan will fail if they do not turn up.'

'I swear it, Grace,' Ellie said, quickly crossing her heart with her finger. 'I'm not a villain like them.' And she hurried off to the Woodyard.

Just before dinner, I went to the passage outside Adam's chambers. I listened at the door to make sure they were still within and then hid round the corner. When I heard their door open, I walked along so as to pass by as they left, as if by sheer coincidence.

'I am pleased to see you out and about,' I gushed. 'Are you feeling better?' It gave me grim satisfaction to see that they both looked very pale and Sylvia was clutching her husband's arm as if she would fall down without its support.

'Thank you, Lady Grace,' said Adam. He tried to do one of his ingratiating bows but his belly must have hurt too much, for he only managed a small bob of the head. 'As you know, we awoke this morning with the puking. It is surely just that we are not used to the wonderful food that is served at Court, being only humble subjects of Her Majesty.'

We walked together in the direction of the Great Hall.

'What happy chance that you are a skilled apothecary,' I said. 'It is easy for you to mix up a curative potion.'

'Well, no, actually . . . ' mumbled Adam. 'I mean, I will, of course, as soon as I feel able—'

'You surprise me, sir,' I cut in. 'I had thought you would already have done so. Unless' – I wrung my hands dramatically – 'perhaps your inability to act is because you are cursed.'

Sylvia let out a small moan, and I saw Adam grimace as she dug her nails into his arm.

'Yes,' I went on, enjoying myself hugely, 'it could be a jinx. A jinx that makes you ill and stops your brain from finding a cure.'

Adam clutched at his pendant. 'You believe in such things as well,' he whispered.

We had reached the doors to the Great Hall now. I nodded gravely. 'Indeed, and if what you told me was right and there *were* gypsies at the fair, then there were probably jinxes and curses flying about all over the place!'

I left them in the doorway, clutching each other and their talismans, and went in for dinner. I saw them stagger in a few moments later. They sat down at a table, took some wine and drank deeply, then refilled their goblets, eyes darting fearfully all over the place.

I will now leave my hiding place behind the cider press, for the smell is beginning to put me off apples for ever. I hope Ellie has fulfilled her mission. I am impatient for Adam's audience with the Queen this afternoon. It is only an hour away but it feels like a day!

Later that day

I am sitting under a tree in the park of St James.

Philip, Henri and Ivan are running around, barking with the excitement of being outdoors.

After the noontide meal the Maids of Honour and Ladies-in-Waiting were summoned to the Queen's Presence Chamber to attend Her Majesty. I sat on my cushion with great anticipation. My plan was about to unfold . . .

We were the only ones present apart from several of the Gentlemen of the Guard. I saw some curious looks pass between the ladies. The Queen entered from her Privy Chamber.

'We expect several visitors,' she told us.

At that the outer door opened and in came Lady Sarah. It was the first time she has ventured out since the fire. Mrs Champernowne and Mr Cheshire walked by her sides. She was wearing her newest gown, a pretty thing of pale green damask, but her ruff was left well open at her throat so that it would not press on the burns there. The mark on her face was pink still, but the skin looked healthy and I felt sure that the burn would ultimately leave no mark.

The Queen smiled benevolently as we all rushed to embrace our fellow Maid. Then she called for our attention. 'Adam the Apothecary and his wife will be with us soon,' she said. 'He believes he is coming to advise us on health matters and you may ask him what you will. But we are all going to be playing a part as if we were acting in a play. You are to remain calm and impassive as statues, no matter what occurs. Follow my lead and mark this. Do not cast your eye upon anything strange that may appear, and know that you are safe throughout – I give you my word. I put this charge upon you. Can you do it?'

We nodded our heads and made our curtsies.

Her Majesty went over to Sarah. 'This will be hardest for you, my dear,' she said kindly. 'But I know you can do it for me.'

Sarah looked a little apprehensive but she nodded and curtsied to the Queen.

We took to our cushions again and the page soon announced the arrival of Adam and Sylvia.

They looked much improved after their meal. I think they had taken courage from the wine they had imbibed. They sat on little wooden stools after bowing deeply to Her Majesty. Adam cast his eyes confidently around the room. He had a large bag with him that chinked as he put it down. It must be full of his salves and ointments. The thought of selling potions to rich courtiers seemed to have driven the fears from his head for the moment.

Sylvia sat proudly by his side. She was making herself at home at Court, acting like the Queen of Sheba.

Adam was unbearably smug with all the attention he was receiving from the twittering ladies around him. They could hardly wait their turn to ply him with questions about rough skin, whitlows and even toenails. I listened as he advised each one, selling potion after potion. I was boiling with anger at his arrogance, but as the minutes passed, my anger gave way to nervous flutters of the belly. There was no sign of Rosa. Supposing she did not want to comply – or could not? Adam and his accomplice would walk free.

'This puts me in mind of my travels through the Mughal Empire,' the apothecary was telling us. 'I journeyed there to find the root of the sarsaparilla, but news of my coming reached the Emperor Akbar. Naturally he summoned me to appear at his Court, where his ladies made much of me . . .'

As he spoke, I caught the slight movement of a wall hanging at the far end of the Presence Chamber. My heart began to beat wildly as I saw, out of the corner of my eye, a pale figure step from behind it. Adam could not see it for it was behind him. I gave a quick glance when his eyes were not on me. Ellie had completed her mission to perfection and transformed Rosa into a truly wondrous spectre, pale as death in skin and dress. Rosa's eyes shone like two dark demons from Hell in her whitened face. Grey voile floated round her, wafting gently in the breeze from the window. It was a perfect scene! I could almost believe the old woman really *had* been summoned from beyond the grave to terrify us. It makes me shiver even to write of it. How the others kept their countenance I know not! Nothing but a royal command could have done it.

Adam and Sylvia had still not seen the ghost. Adam was looking straight at me now and I hoped I had not given anything away in my face. I put my chin in my hand and pretended to be fascinated by the nonsense the pompous man was relating.

The ghost walked silently up behind him as he burbled on. I felt I could hardly breathe!

'... and I gave them instant cures for their warts and soothed their babies' fevers and ... and ...'

Silently Rosa walked round so that she now appeared in front of them. Adam and Sylvia had been so intent on the Queen that it must have seemed to them as if she had appeared out of thin air. Adam faltered, and his jaw dropped open. Sylvia turned pale.

I tingled with delight. My plan was working!

'Do continue with your tale, Adam,' the Queen said smoothly. 'We are all ears.'

'But, M–My Liege . . .' The words stumbled from Adam's trembling lips. 'Do you not see the horror before you?' He lurched to his feet, knocking over his stool, and searched our faces. 'Surely you *all* see it . . .'

We put on our most blank expressions, and looked anywhere but at Rosa. I was so proud of my fellow courtiers.

'What is this horror of which you speak?' asked Her Majesty, as if puzzled. 'Do I have a spot on the end of my nose? If so, I am sure you will find me the perfect salve for it.'

If I had not been so tense, I would have exploded with mirth. The Queen is a wonderful actor.

'Indeed you have not, Your Majesty,' faltered Adam. 'I would never dare to suggest . . . it's just that I thought I saw . . . but, no, it is nothing . . .' He picked up his stool and sat again, but his hands were trembling. I could see that he was trying not to look at Rosa, who stood there, shaking her head sorrowfully at him.

'That is a most interesting talisman round your neck,' I said brightly to him. 'The pentangle, I think you told me.'

'A most valuable protection,' Adam managed to answer. His eyes darted wildly about the room, but always came back to rest on the ghostly figure before him. Sylvia sat as if transfixed, eyes wide and hands clutching her stool in terror. Small whimpers escaped her lips.

In faith, even though my companions did not know what was going on, they now joined in with the spirit of the moment. (What a pun I have made!)

'We must be vigilant.' Lucy nodded around the group. 'Since the fair I have carried a rabbit's foot everywhere with me to keep ill luck away – even to my bed.'

'Ill luck is one thing,' I blurted out like a hysterical girl. 'But I have heard that the curse of a murdered man is proof against any talisman in the world. The murderer will be jinxed to his life's end.'

Rosa nodded slowly. Sylvia gave a strangled cry.

'Do you remember the ghost at Medenham Manor?' Sarah put in. 'We were told it would plague the Earl until all wrongs were righted.'

Well done, Sarah, I thought.

'Spirits only rest when the truth is revealed,' put in Mary Shelton wisely.

Rosa raised an arm and pointed straight at the

apothecary. This was too much for Adam and Sylvia. They fell to their knees in front of her.

'Forgive me, spirit,' sobbed Adam, wringing his hands. 'I swear I did not mean to kill you. I only set fire to the tent to scare you out so that I could take your haoma resin. I beseech you, Rosa, take away this torturing curse that rots our bellies, and leave us be.'

The audience sat open-mouthed. They had not expected this turn of events, I warrant. I wanted to run round the room cheering, but I kept my seat. Her Majesty rose from her chair with a terrible calmness. She stood before Adam.

'You miserable wretch,' she said icily. 'By your own admission you are responsible for the deadly fire at St Bartholomew's Fair?'

'I am,' groaned Adam. 'And I am paying dearly for it. My life is over.'

'I had nothing to do with the fire,' screeched his cowardly wife. Gone was her soft, floaty voice. 'It was—'

'Silence!' shouted the Queen. 'You are as guilty as your husband. Guards, seize them!'

Daniel Cheshire was the first to obey. I could see that he wanted to do a lot more than merely arrest the man who had harmed his love!

'And now for you, Rosa.' And to Adam and

 182

Sylvia's utter astonishment, the Queen walked over and took the ghost by the hand. The ghost curtsied politely before her. 'You have played your part to perfection. And my compliments to your dresser!'

It was a wonderful moment, but Adam was suddenly enraged. He struggled against Mr Cheshire's grasp.

'I have been tricked!' he shouted. 'Tricked into a false confession!'

'We had nothing to do with any fire,' snapped his wife. 'My husband spoke in haste to pacify a spirit we thought was out to harm us, that is all.'

'Indeed,' said the Queen. 'Then how do you account for Rosa's box, containing her special herb, being found in your chamber?'

This silenced Sylvia, but a cunning look came into Adam's eyes.

'Do not believe anything that lying woman says,' he growled, pointing to Rosa. 'For she is a gypsy!'

There was a gasp from the onlookers.

'How dare you!' thundered Her Majesty. 'Are you accusing me of harbouring a gypsy at my Court? Guards, take them away!'

When the prisoners had been dragged from our sight, Her Majesty rose. We all bowed and curtsied.

'And now let us repair to the Tilting Yard,' she said, smiling. 'We have provided enough entertainment for ourselves. It is time for Mr Somers and his troupe to divert us instead.' She walked to the door and turned.

'Lady Grace,' she called to me. 'I meant to tell you. The cure you suggested to me earlier has had wonderful effect. Thank you.'

And I felt so happy I could have burst!

It was not long before we were seated on the stand of wooden seats before a small makeshift stage in the Tilting Yard. I was honoured to be next to Her Majesty, who sat in her carved chair, shaded from the brightness of the afternoon sun by a gold canopy. There were smiles all round when Lady Sarah appeared on the arm of Daniel Cheshire, and the Queen beckoned to her to sit on her other side. Truly we Maids are like a family to her.

Sarah held her head high. And there was something different in her eyes — a sort of contentment that I had not seen before.

'Mr Cheshire has been Sarah's best medicine, I vow,' the Queen said in a low voice when she saw me looking. 'But at what cost? Has he not had the salve applied to his own burns?'

Daniel Cheshire's hands were still swathed in bandages.

'He will not let anyone touch them, Your

Majesty,' I answered. 'Sarah told me he cherishes his scars, for they will always remind him of how precious her life is to him.'

And for once that did not sound too silly, even to me.

'Then he had better bide with her,' remarked the Queen. 'For the marks of a former love can be an awkward reminder.'

This was something – coming from Her Majesty! She is usually like an angry terrier at the heels of any man who comes to wed one of her Maids. I had the impression the Queen did not altogether dislike Sarah's suitor!

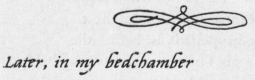

Later, in my bedchamber

Well, I had thought to finish my tale peacefully under the trees while the Queen's dogs amused themselves. However, it seems that my furry little charges did not like the idea of their mistress being stationary for too long, for they suddenly ran round me, yapping loudly as I wrote, and would not let me be. Now they are back in their own room, worn out by the walk I have given them. I expect they are asleep on their cushions by now.

Now, where was I? Of course – Her Majesty had just amazed me by casting a benevolent eye on Lady Sarah and Mr Cheshire.

With that all settled, I then wondered how Ellie was faring. I glanced across from my seat by the Queen to where the tiring women were standing. Ellie is not very tall and I was anxious that she should have a good view. I need not have worried. Fran and Olwen had let her stand in front of them, and she gave me a merry wave. The Queen glanced at us both and smiled. I wanted to hug her for turning a blind eye to our friendship – but of course she is my monarch and I never would. I must see Ellie later. I have not had a chance to thank her for creating such a good ghost!

A funny thing happened just before the entertainment began. There was a clattering behind us, and I turned to see Mrs Champernowne's large bum sticking up. She was grovelling around on the ground picking up beads, which was not easy for such a large lady in such a small space. I tried to help.

'No, Grace,' she said breathlessly. 'Only I can touch them. My bracelet broke and the beads must go back in a certain order for it is a charm to ward off evil. I bought it at the fair. Lack-a-day, I hope I have not brought ill luck upon us!'

Poor Mrs Champernowne. I left her to it.

There was a roll of drums and Mr Somers's troupe burst into view. It was a glorious sight, with the brightly coloured tumblers flipping about the Tilting Yard to the sound of pipes and tambours. Our heads whirled with the speed of it. At each human pyramid and clever tumble I heard Mrs Champernowne gasp and clutch her bracelet, willing nothing to go wrong.

But Masou did not appear. I began to worry, thinking he must be in disgrace and that was why he had been so secretive for the last few days. Then suddenly there was a thunderous applause, led by the Queen herself, and Masou came into view – on his hands. He leaped to his feet in front of Her Majesty, with a most elaborate bow, winking at me as he did.

'My Liege,' he declared, 'I present for your eyes a trick that has never before been attempted. A trick that you would not believe possible unless you were here to witness it.'

The crowd murmured eagerly. So that was why Masou had been so elusive, I thought. He had been perfecting his act and wanted to keep it secret even from me – *especially* from me! He knows I would not have been able to resist the challenge of working out his method. I was determined that I would see through his trick, whatever it might be.

With that, little Gypsy Pete bounded up to him, chest puffed out, and took his bow, grinning from ear to ear. Come to think of it, I wonder that he is called Gypsy Pete – for he has no gypsy blood, I think. But who knows? Anyhow, the crowd love him almost as much as they love Masou and they roared their approval.

'I must beg absolute silence,' intoned Masou solemnly. It was all nonsense, I am sure, but it added to the effect. You could have heard a pin drop – or one of Mrs Champernowne's beads, Heaven forfend!

Gypsy Pete stood like a soldier in the centre of the stage and Mr Somers tossed a large red velvet cloth to Masou. Masou made a great show of parading this round the stage, waving it about him like a flag. (So *that* was what he had been practising with the old sheet.) Then, with a flourish, he suddenly threw the cloth over Gypsy Pete. It took his shape, then slowly sunk to the stage.

'Abou Kassam. Abou Kassoo,' cried Masou, and flung away the cloth. To our astonishment Gypsy Pete had vanished, and in his place was a cloud of white doves, rising into the air!

We gasped out loud and Mrs Champernowne clutched my shoulder. 'God save us, Grace,' she muttered. 'I pray the poor boy is not gone for good thanks to me!'

But Masou flung out an arm towards a tall tree in the corner of the Tilting Yard. And, as the doves flew away, there was Gypsy Pete, on a high branch, waving and smiling for all to see. Mrs Champernowne nearly fainted with relief. The Queen stood, and then we all did, and I should think our cheering could be heard all over the park of St James.

I watched the doves soaring overhead. They were Her Majesty's gift from the Spanish Ambassador, I was sure – and I could see by her face that she was well pleased to let them have their freedom. I expect there will be room for them in the dovecotes of Whitehall.

Now this mystery is solved and all is well, except for one thing: I have no idea how Masou's trick was done! Curses! Though perhaps there has been enough talk of those.

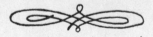

A few moments later

A great noise just erupted in the passageway outside my chamber. It is Lady Jane and Lady

Sarah, and they are shouting at each other. Now that Sarah has her fair looks back Jane obviously feels there is no need to be nice to her any more.

We are back to normal.

Hurrah!

GLOSSARY

aiglet – the metal tip of a lace, which you thread through the hole

amulet – an object thought to carry protection against evil

apothecary – an Elizabethan chemist

basil – a leafy green herb with a strong smell and flavour

Bedlam – the major asylum for the insane in London during Elizabethan times – the name came from Bethlem Hospital

damask – a beautiful, self-patterned silk cloth woven in Flanders. It originally came from Damascus – hence the name

daybooke – a book in which you would record your sins each day so that you could pray about them. The idea of keeping a diary or journal grew out of this. Grace is using hers as a journal

Deputy Naperer – second in command of the Royal table linens

Don Guerau de Spes – the Spanish ambassador to London, said to be involved in many conspiracies to dethrone Queen Elizabeth

doublet – a close-fitting padded jacket worn by men

elfshot – a stone, possibly an arrowhead, thought to have been used by elves and providing protection against evil magic

garlic – a plant, the bulb of which contains small white cloves with a strong smell and taste used for seasoning and for medicinal purposes

ginger – a root with a pungent flavour used in cooking and for medicinal purposes

goat's rue – a little pink or purple flower much like the flower of a pea plant

gudgeon – a small, bottom-dwelling fish

hex – a spell or charm, or to practice witchcraft

kirtle – the skirt section of an Elizabethan dress

Lady-in-Waiting – one of the ladies who helped to look after the Queen and who kept her company

laudanum – a medicine containing opium

Maid of Honour – a younger girl who helped to look after the Queen like a Lady-in-Waiting

manchet bread – white bread

Mary Shelton – one of Queen Elizabeth's Maids of Honour (a Maid of Honour of this name really did exist, see below). Most Maids of Honour were not officially 'ladies' (like Lady Grace) but they had to be of born of gentry

nosegay – a small bunch of flowers held up to the nose to avoid the foul smells that were abundant in Elizabethan times

partlet – a very fine embroidered false top, which covered just the shoulders and the upper chest

penner – a small leather case which would attach to a belt. It was used for holding quills, ink, knife and any other equipment needed for writing

pentangle – a pentagram, a star with five points

pickage – the fee paid to set up a stall at a fair

Presence Chamber – the room where Queen Elizabeth received people

Privy Chamber – the room where the Queen would receive people in private

Privy Garden – Queen Elizabeth's private garden

on progress – term used when the Queen was touring parts of her realm. It was a kind of summer holiday for her

pursuivant – one who pursues someone else

Queen's Guard – these were more commonly known as the Gentlemen Pensioners – young noblemen who guarded the Queen from physical attacks

ratsbane – rat poison, containing arsenic

Secretary Cecil – William Cecil, an administrator for the Queen (was later made Lord Burghley)

Shaitan – the Islamic word for Satan, though it means a trickster and a liar rather than the ultimate evil

small beer – weak beer

stomacher – a heavily embroidered or jewelled piece for the centre front of a bodice

Stone Gallery – a part of Whitehall no longer standing that ran between several main buildings and the Privy Garden

sweetmeats – sweets

talisman – similar to an amulet, an object with carvings to ward off evil

Tilting Yard – area where knights in armour would

joust or 'tilt' (i.e. ride at each other on horseback with lances)

tiring woman – a woman who helped a lady to dress

tumbler – acrobat

waterman – a man who rowed a ferry boat on the Thames – he was a kind of Elizabethan cab driver

whitlow – an infection around fingernails and toenails that usually happens when the cutical is damaged

woodwild – crazy, mad

THE FACT BEHIND THE FICTION

In 1485 Queen Elizabeth I's grandfather, Henry Tudor, won the battle of Bosworth Field against Richard III and took the throne of England. He was known as Henry VII. He had two sons, Arthur and Henry. Arthur died while still a boy, so when Henry VII died in 1509, Elizabeth's father came to the throne and England got an eighth king called Henry – the notorious one who had six wives.

Wife number one – Catherine of Aragon – gave Henry one daughter called Mary (who was brought up as a Catholic), but no living sons. To Henry VIII this was a disaster, because nobody believed a queen could ever govern England. He needed a male heir.

Henry wanted to divorce Catherine so he could marry his pregnant mistress, Anne Boleyn. The Pope, the head of the Catholic Church, wouldn't allow him to annul his marriage, so Henry broke with the Catholic Church and set up the Protestant Church of England – or the Episcopal Church, as it's known in the USA.

Wife number two – Anne Boleyn – gave Henry another daughter, Elizabeth (who was brought up as a Protestant). When Anne then miscarried a baby boy, Henry decided he'd better get somebody new, so he accused Anne of infidelity and had her executed.

Wife number three – Jane Seymour – gave Henry a son called Edward, and died of childbed fever a couple of weeks later.

Wife number four – Anne of Cleves – had no children. It was a diplomatic marriage and Henry didn't fancy her, so she agreed to a divorce (wouldn't you?).

Wife number five – Catherine Howard – had no children either. Like Anne Boleyn, she was accused of infidelity and executed.

Wife number six – Catherine Parr – also had no children. She did manage to outlive Henry, though, but only by the skin of her teeth. Nice guy, eh?

Henry VIII died in 1547, and in accordance with the rules of primogeniture (whereby the first-born son inherits from his father), the person who succeeded him was the boy Edward. He became Edward VI. He was strongly Protestant, but died young in 1553.

Next came Catherine of Aragon's daughter, Mary, who became Mary I, known as Bloody Mary. She was strongly Catholic, married Philip II of Spain in a diplomatic match, but died childless five years later. She also burned a lot of Protestants for the good of their souls.

Finally, in 1558, Elizabeth came to the throne. She reigned until her death in 1603. She played the marriage game – that is, she kept a lot of important and influential men hanging on in hopes of marrying her – for a long time. At one time it looked as if she would marry her favourite, Robert Dudley, Earl of Leicester. She didn't though, and I think she probably never intended to get married – would you, if you'd had a dad like hers? So she never had any children.

She was an extraordinary and brilliant woman, and during her reign, England first started to become important as a world power. Sir Francis Drake sailed round the world – raiding the Spanish colonies of South America for loot as he went. And one of Elizabeth's favourite courtiers, Sir Walter Raleigh, tried to plant the first English colony in North America – at the site of Roanoke in 1585. It failed, but the idea stuck.

The Spanish King Philip II tried to conquer England in 1588. He sent a huge fleet of 150 ships, known as the Invincible Armada, to do it. It failed miserably – defeated by Drake at the head of the English fleet – and most of the ships were wrecked trying to sail home. There were many other great

Elizabethans, too – including William Shakespeare and Christopher Marlowe.

After her death, Elizabeth was succeeded by James VI of Scotland, who became James I of England and Scotland. He was almost the last eligible person available! He was the son of Mary Queen of Scots, who was Elizabeth's cousin, via Henry VIII's sister.

His son was Charles I – the King who was beheaded after losing the English Civil War.

The stories about Lady Grace Cavendish are set in the years 1569 and 1570, when Elizabeth was thirty-six and still playing the marriage game for all she was worth. The Ladies-in-Waiting and Maids of Honour at her Court weren't servants – they were companions and friends, supplied from upper-class families. Not all of them were officially 'ladies' – only those with titled husbands or fathers; in fact, many of them were unmarried younger daughters sent to Court to find themselves a nice rich lord to marry.

All the Lady Grace Mysteries are invented, but some of the characters in the stories are real people – Queen Elizabeth herself, of course, and Mrs Champernowne and Mary Shelton as well. There never was a Lady Grace Cavendish (as far as we know!) – but there were plenty of girls like her at Elizabeth's Court. The real Mary Shelton foolishly made fun of the Queen herself on one occasion – and got slapped in the face by Elizabeth for her trouble! But most of the time, the Queen seems to have been protective and kind to her Maids of Honour. She was very strict about boyfriends, though. There was one simple rule for boyfriends in those days: you couldn't have one. No boyfriends at all. You would get married to a person your parents chose for you and that was that. Of course, the girls often had other ideas!

Later on in her reign, the Queen had a full-scale secret service run by her great spymaster, Sir Francis Walsingham. His men, who hunted down priests and assassins, were called 'pursuivants'. There are also tantalizing hints that Elizabeth may have had her own personal sources of information – she certainly was very well informed, even when her counsellors tried to keep her in the dark. And who knows whom she might have recruited to find things out for her? There may even have been a Lady Grace Cavendish, after all!

A note on St Bartholomew's Fair

St Bartholomew's Fair was one of the biggest fairs in England. It was held every August around the Feast of St Bartholomew.

The fair came about in 1133 because of a medieval Masou character. His name was Rahere and he was a member of the Court of King Henry I. He spent his days performing at banquets and making jests for his King, just like Masou does for Queen Elizabeth. Then Rahere became a monk, and after seeing a vision of St Bartholomew, he founded St Bartholomew's Church, Barts Hospital and the fair at Smithfield in the City of London. Although he had become a monk it was said that he still entertained the fairgoers with his capers. There are stories that his ghost haunts the church even today, as a shadowy hooded figure whose sandaled feet can be heard on the flagstones. He brushes past astonished visitors and fades slowly into thin air.

St Bartholomew's Fair began as a cloth fair – one of the roads leading off Smithfield is still called 'Cloth Fair' – but soon all sorts of traders were putting up their stalls. The fair prospered as it was near the port of London, so traders from other parts of the country and Europe could easily bring their goods to sell, and it took place in summer – a good time of year for people to travel to it. The church and the hospital also prospered as they received toll payments from the fair.

Although the fair was set up for trade, many people began to go for the entertainments – such as fortune-tellers, acrobats, strolling players and fire-eaters. If accounts are to be believed, over the centuries some amazing sights could be seen at St Bartholomew's Fair, including the 'eight-foot-tall' (2.44m) woman, the man with one head and two bodies, and a fortune-telling horse. Samuel Pepys, the seventeenth-century diarist, even wrote about a famous acrobat, Scaramouch, who danced on a tightrope while pushing a wheelbarrow in front of him containing two children and a dog, and with a duck sitting on his head! One of the most extraordinary stories comes from 1817 and tells of Toby, 'the real learned pig' who, despite having his eyes covered with twenty handkerchiefs, could tell the time and pick out a card from a pack.

In the early years of the eighteenth century there was a Ferris wheel, which was known then as a Whirligig. A journalist of the time wrote that children were 'locked up in Flying Coaches who insensibly climb'd upwards . . . being once Elevated to a certain height come down again according to the Circular Motion of the Sphere they move in'. In other words it was a bit like the London Eye.

Not all spectacles at the fair were pleasant. In 1315 Sir William Wallace was dragged to Smithfield behind a horse, and hanged, drawn and quartered in sight of jostling fairgoers.

The fair was also a magnet for crime. The great gathering of people made the fair a prime place for pickpockets to work, and fights often broke out, just like the one Grace witnessed. A gang called Lady Holland's Mob robbed visitors, beat passers-by with heavy sticks, and threw things at anyone who came to their window to see what all the noise was about.

By the 1850s the sideshows had all been banned in an attempt to stop this violence and the fair had dwindled to nothing more than a few gingerbread stalls. Eventually the Lord Mayor came to proclaim the opening of the fair and found there was no fair to open! A sad end to a great tradition that had lasted over seven hundred years.

Sewering, W. 2000: Herz, Kunstherz oder Themenpark? In Rauch *et al.* (eds), 47–58.

Sharp, I. and Flinspach, D. 1995: Women in Germany from division to unification. In Lewis, D. and McKenzie, J. (eds), 173–95.

Siebenhaar, K. (ed.) 2000: *Kulturhandbuch Berlin. Geschichte und Gegenwart von A–Z.* Berlin: Bastelmann und Sieben.

Smith, E.O. 1994: *The German Economy.* London and New York: Routledge.

Smith, G., Paterson, W.E. and Merkl, P.H. (eds) 1989: *Developments in West German Politics.* London: Macmillan.

Smyser, W.R. 1993: *The German Economy: Colossus at the Crossroads,* 2nd edn. Harlow: Longman.

Sontheimer, M. 1999: *Berlin, Berlin. Der Umzug in die Hauptstadt.* Hamburg: Hoffmann und Campe.

Speakman, F. and Speakman, C. 1992: *The Green Guide to Germany.* London: Green Print.

Staritz, D. 1996: *Geschichte der DDR.* Frankfurt am Main: Suhrkamp.

Statistisches Bundesamt (ed.) 1997: *Datenreport 1997.* Bonn: Bundeszentrale für politische Bildung.

Statistisches Jahrbuch (ed.) 1999: Statistisches Jahrbuch für die Bundesrepublik Deutschland und für das Ausland. Wiesbaden and Stuttgart: Statistisches Bundesamt/Metzler-Poeschel Verlag. Published as CD-ROM.

Staunton, D. 1999: No jokes please we're German, advertising students told. *Guardian* 20 June, 16.

Steele, J. 2000: Fortress Europe confronts the unthinkable. *Guardian* 30 October 17.

Stern 1995: In Hülle und Fülle. *Stern* (27), 21.

Stevenson, P. (ed.) 1997: *The German Language and the Real World: Sociolinguistic, Cultural, and Pragmatic Perspectives on Contemporary German,* revised edn. Oxford: Clarendon Press.

Steyer, C-D. 2000: Der Konflikt mit den Bauern ist im Nationalpark vertagt. *Der Tagesspiegel* 7 April, 18.

Story, J. 1996: Finanzplatz Deutschland: national or European response to internationalisation? *German Politics* 5(3), 371–94.

Streeck, J. 1995: Ethnomethodologische Differenzen im Ost-West-Verhältnis. In Czyzewski *et al.* (eds), 430–6.

Strohschneider, S. 1997: Eine Nation, zwei Arten des Denkens. *Psychologie Heute* March, 30–5.

Sturm, R. 1997a: Aufgabenstrukturen, Kompetenzen und Finanzierung. In Gabriel, O.W. and Holtmann, E. (eds), 619–58.

Sturm, R. 1997b: Arbeit und Wirtschaft. In Gabriel, O.W. and Holtmann, E. (eds) 659–79.

Süß, W. and Rytlewski, R. (eds) 1999: *Berlin. Die Hauptstadt. Vergangenheit und Zukunft einer europäischen Metropole.* Berlin: Nicolai.

Taylor, R. 1997: *Berlin and its Culture: A Historical Portrait.* New Haven, CT and London: Yale University Press.

Traynor, I. 1998a: Pornography test case for internet providers. *Guardian,* 13 May, 14.

Traynor, I. 1998b: Disaffected east turning its back on Kohl the unifier. *Guardian* 23 September, 17.

Traynor, I. 1999a: Germany champions women in the home. *Guardian* 19 June, 16.

Traynor, I. 1999b: German Catholics in uproar at Pope's ban on abortion advice. *Guardian* 19 June, 16.

Leonardy, U. 1999: The institutional structures of German federalism. In Jeffery, C. (ed.), 3–22.

Lewis, D. 1995: The GDR. *Wende* and legacy. In Lewis, D. and McKenzie, J. (eds), 52–73.

Lewis, D. and McKenzie, J. (eds) 1995: *The New Germany: Social, Political and Cultural Challenges of Unification.* Exeter: University of Exeter Press.

Ludz, P.C. and Kuppe, J. 1975: *DDR Handbuch.* Köln: Wissenschaft und Politik.

Lütz, S. 2000: From managed to market capitalism? German finance in transition. *German Politics* 9(2), 149–70.

McElvoy, A. 1992: *The Saddled Cow: East Germany's Life and Legacy.* London: Faber and Faber.

Maier, H. 1989: Die Katholische Kirche in der Bundesrepublik Deutschland. In Weidenfeld, W. and Zimmermann, H. (eds), 165–73.

Malunat, B.M. 1994: Die Umweltpolitik der Bundesrepublik Deutschland. *Aus Politik und Zeitgeschichte* B49/94, 3–12.

Maretzke, S. and Irmen, E. 1999: Die ostdeutschen Regionen im Wandel. Regionale Aspekte des Transformationsprozesses. *Aus Politik und Zeitgeschichte,* B5/99, 3–99.

Maull, H. 2000: German foreign policy, post-Kosovo: still a civilian power? *German Politics* 9(2), 1–24.

Menze, C. 1996: Zur Geschichte der Universität 1945–1996. *Pädagogische Rundschau* 50, 379–406.

Meyn, H. 1992: *Massenmedien in der Bundesrepublik Deutschland.* Berlin: Colloquium Verlag.

Moeller, M.L. and Maaz, H-J. 1995: *Die Einheit beginnt zu zweit. Ein deutsch-deutsches Zwiegespräch.* Reinbek: Rowohlt.

Mönch, R. 1998: Zwei von drei Häusern wurden korrekt erworben. *Der Tagesspiegel* 16 December.

Müller, B.-D. (ed.) 1991a: *Interkulturelle Wirtschaftskommunikation.* München: iudicium verlag.

Müller, B.-D. 1991b: Die Bedeutung der interkulturellen Kommunikation für die Wirtschaft. In Müller, B.-D. (ed.), 27–52.

Müller-Heidelberg, T., Finckh, U., Narr, W.-D. and Pelzer, M. (eds) 1998: *Grundrechte-Report. Zur Lage der Bürger- und Menschenrechte in Deutschland.* Hamburg: Rowohlt.

Müller-Schneider, T. 1998: Freizeit und Erholung. In Schäfers, B. and Zapf, W. (eds), 221–31.

Nave-Herz, R. 1998: Familie und Verwandschaft. In Schäfers, B. and Zapf, W. (eds), 201–10.

Neather, E. 1995: Education in the new Germany. In Lewis, D. and McKenzie, J. (eds), 148–72.

Neubacher, A. 2000: Abschied vom Monopol. *Der Spiegel* (6) 7 February, 72–3.

Neuweiler, G. 1994: Das gesamtdeutsche Haus für Forschung und Lehre. *Aus Politik und Zeitgeschichte* B25/94, 3–11.

Niebaum, H. and Macha, J. 1999: *Einführung in die Dialektologie des Deutschen.* Tübingen: Max Niemeyer Verlag.

Nissen, S. 1997: Soziale Sicherung. In Gabriel, O.W. and Holtmann, E. (eds), 681–96.

Noelle-Neumann, E., Schulz, W. and Wilke, J. (eds) 2000: *Publizistik. Massenkommunikation.* Frankfurt am Main: Fischer.

Nooteboom, C. 1999: *Allerseelen*. Frankfurt am Main: Suhrkamp.

Nowak, K. 1995: Evangelische Kirche in der DDR. *Geschichte in Wissenschaft und Unterricht* **46**(1), 142–52.

Oppermann, C. 2000: Vereint in Armut und Reichtum. *Die Woche: Wirtschaft* 29 September, 14–15.

Osborn, A. 2000: Official calls for public vote on enlarging EU. *Guardian* 4 September, 12.

Otto, J. 1999: Winners and losers. *Die Zeit* 9 September.

Paterson, T. 2000a: East Germans revive red rite of passage. *Guardian* 1 April, 15.

Paterson, T. 2000b: Row as Holocaust defender wins prize. *Guardian* 1 June, 16.

Paterson, T. 2000c: Schröder condition on EU entry. *Guardian* 19 December, 14

Paterson, W.E. and Southern, D. 1991: *Governing Germany*. Oxford: Blackwell.

Patterson, M. 1995: The German theatre. In Lewis, D. and McKenzie, J. (eds), 259–75.

Patzelt, W.J. 1997: Der Bundesrat. In Gabriel, O.W. and Holtmann, E. (eds), 207–28.

Paul, I. 2000: Gerahmte Kommunikation. Die Inszenierung ost- und westdeutscher Kommunikationserfahrungen im Mediendiskurs. In Auer, P. and Hausendorf, H. (eds), 113–50.

Peacock, A. and Willgerodt, H. (eds) 1989: *Germany's Social Market Economy: Origins and Evolution*. London: Macmillan.

Pfahl-Traughber, A. 1999: *Rechtextremismus in der Bundesrepublik*. München: Verlag C.H. Beck.

Picht, G. 1964: *Die Deutsche Bildungskatastrophe*. Freiburg: Walter.

Plenzdorf, U., Schlesinger, K. and Stade, M. 1995: *Berliner Geschichten*. Frankfurt am Main: Suhrkamp.

Plöhn J. 1997: Die Gerichtsbarkeit. In Gabriel, O.W. and Holtmann, E. (eds), 355–77.

Pogunkte, T. 1997: Politische Parteien. In Gabriel, O.W. and Holtmann, E. (eds), 501–23.

Pohl, I. 1997: Bedeutung sprachlicher Ausdrücke im Wandel. *Der Deutschunterricht* (1), 50–8.

Polenz, P. v. 1993: Die Sprachrevolte in der DDR im Herbst 1989. Ein Forschungsbericht nach drei Jahren vereinter germanistischer Linguistik. *Zeitschrift für germanistische Linguistik* (21), 127–49.

Pötzsch, H. 1998: *Deutsche Geschichte von 1945 bis zur Gegenwart. Die Entwicklung der beiden deutschen Staaten*. München: Olzog.

Presse- und Informationsamt des Landes Berlin 1992: *Berlin Handbuch. Das Lexikon der Bundeshauptstadt*. Berlin: FAB Verlag.

Pritchard, R. 1998: Education transformed? The east German school system since the *Wende*. *German Politics* **7**(3), 126–46.

Probst, L. (ed.) 1999: *Differenz in der Einheit*. Berlin: Christoph Links Verlag.

Prützel-Thomas, M. 1993: The abortion issue and the Federal Constitutional Court. *German Politics* **2**(3), 467–84.

Raff, D. 1985: *Deutsche Geschichte vom Alten Reich zur Zweiten Republik*. München: Max Hueber Verlag.

Rauch, Y. v. and Visscher, J. (eds) 2000: *Der Potsdamer Platz. Urbane Architektur für das neue Berlin*. Berlin: Jovis.

Reiher, R. 1997: Dreiraum- versus Dreizimmerwohnung. Zum Sprachgebrauch der Ostdeutschen. *Der Deutschunterricht* (1), 42–9.

Richie, A. 1999: *Faust's Metropolis: A History of Berlin*. London: HarperCollins.

Richter, G. 1999: Enttäuschte Erwartungen? Liebesbeziehungen zwischen Ost und West. In Probst, L. (ed.), 152–62.

Richter, M.W. 1994: Exiting the GDR: political movements and parties between democratization and westernization. In Hancock, M.D. and Welsh, H.A. (eds), 93–138.

Roberts, G.K. 1997: *Party Politics in the New Germany*. London: Pinter.

Rohlfs, H.-H. and Schäfer, U. (eds) 1997: *Jahrbuch der Bundesrepublik Deutschland 1997*, 12th edn. München: Deutscher Taschenbuch Verlag.

Rost-Roth, M. 1997: Language in intercultural communication. In Stevenson, P. (ed.), 171–206.

Roth, A. and Frajman, M. 1998: *The Goldapple Guide to Jewish Berlin*. Berlin: Goldapple.

Rother, K. 1994: Gedanken zur Gliederung und Terminologie Deutschlands. Das Beispiel 'Mitteldeutschland'. *Geographische Rundschau* **46**(12), 728–30.

Rüdig, W. 2000: Phasing out nuclear energy in Germany. *German Politics* **9**(3), 43–80.

Russ, C.V. 1994: *The German Language Today: A Linguistic Introduction*. London and New York: Routledge.

Salzen, C. von 2000: Erschreckende Ahnungslosigkeit über Holocaust. *Der Tagesspiegel* 18 February, 5.

Sandford, J. 1995: The German media. In Lewis, D. and McKenzie, J. (eds), 199–219.

Schäfers, B. 1998: *Politischer Atlas Deutschland. Gesellschaft, Wirtschaft, Staat*. Bonn: Dietz Verlag.

Schäfers, B. and Zapf, W. (eds) 1998: *Handwörterbuch zur Gesellschaft Deutschlands*. Opladen: Leske + Budrich.

Schlicht, U. 2000: Hotel Mama begünstigt das Studium zu Hause. *Der Tagesspiegel* 27 September, 36.

Schlicht, U. and Törne, L.v. 1999: Eine Frage der Scheine. *Der Tagesspiegel*. 30 October, 2.

Schluchter, W. 1994: Die Hochschulen in Ostdeutschland vor und nach der Einigung. *Aus Politik und Zeitgeschichte* B25/94, 12–22.

Schneider, H.-P. 1999: German unification and the federal system: the challenge of reform. In Jeffery, C. (ed.), 58–84.

Schneider, P. 1999: *Eduards Heimkehr*. Berlin: Rowohlt.

Schröder, U. 1996: Corporate governance in Germany: the changing role of the banks. *German Politics* **5**(3), 356–70.

Schroeder, K. 1998: *Der SED-Staat: Partei, Staat und Gesellschaft 1949–1990*. München: Propyläen Taschenbuch/Carl Hanser Verlag.

Schuster, F. 2000: Den Standort Thüringen stärken. Regierungserklärung des Ministers für Wirtschaft, Arbeit und Infrastruktur vom 16. März 2000. *http://www.thueringen.de/pm/pm2–1603.htm*

Schütz, E. (ed.) 1999: *Text der Stadt. Reden von Berlin. Literatur und Metropole seit 1989*. Berlin: Weidler.

Schwehn, K.J. 1998: Der FDP fehlen die Frauen. *Der Tagesspiegel* 28 August, 2.

Seifert, W. 1997: Integration von Ausländern. *Statistisches Bundesamt*, 579–89.

Seils, C. 2000: Die Birthler-Behörde. *Die Woche: Wirtschaft* 29 September, 10.

Senatsverwaltung für Stadtentwicklung (ed.) 2000: *Berlin. Zehn Jahre Transformation und Modernisierung*. Berlin.

Traynor, I. and Walker, M. 1998: Herr Mittel Europa. *Guardian* 25 September, 21.

Turner, H.A. 1987: *The Two Germanies since 1945*. New Haven, CT and London: Yale University Press.

Weber, H. 1991: *DDR: Grundriss der Geschichte 1945–1990*. Hannover: Fackelträger.

Weber, H. 1993: Die Geschichte der DDR. Versuch einer vorläufigen Bilanz. In Henke, K.-D. (ed.), 19–34.

Wehling, H.-G. 1989: *Politische Kultur in der DDR*. Stuttgart: Kohlhammer.

Weidenfeld, W. and Korte, K.-R. 1991: *Handwörterbuch zur deutschen Einheit*. Bonn: Campus Verlag.

Weidenfeld, W. and Zimmermann, H. (eds) 1989: *Deutschland-Handbuch. Eine doppelte Bilanz 1949–1989*. Bonn: Bundeszentrale für politische Bildung.

Weingarten, S. and Wellershoff, M. 1999: Fördert, was ihr kriegen könnt. *Der Spiegel* (47) 22 November, 84–104.

Welsh, H.A. 1994: The collapse of communism in eastern Europe and the GDR: Evolution, revolution, and diffusion. In Hancock, M.D. and Welsh, H.A. 17–34.

Wendt, I. 1990: *Notopfer Berlin*. Reprint of 1956 edn. Berlin: Fannei & Watz.

Wensierski, P. 2001: Mir kann nichts passieren. *Der Spiegel* (3) 15 January, 56–8.

Wickel, H.-P. 2000: *Ratgeber Wehrdienst*. Hamburg: Rowohlt.

Wiesenthal, H. 1998: Post-unification dissatisfaction, or Why are so many east Germans unhappy with the new political system? *German Politics* 7(2), 1–30.

Wilke, J. 1996: Multimedia. Strukturwandel durch neue Kommunikationstechnologien. *Aus Politik und Zeitgeschichte*, B32/96, 3–12.

Wilke, S. 2000: Die *Lausitz* will vom Rand zum Herz Europas werden. *Der Tagesspiegel* 25 March, 22.

Wilkens, E. 1989: Die Evangelische Kirche in Deutschland. In Weidenfeld, W. and Zimmermann, H. (eds), 185–92.

Winkel, O. 1996: Wertewandel und Politikwandel. *Aus Politik und Zeitgeschichte* B52–53/96; 13–25.

Wise, M.Z. 1998: *Capital Dilemma Germany's Search for a New Architecture of Democracy*. New York: Princeton Architectural Press.

Wolf, R. 1995: Interaktive Fallen auf dem Weg zum vorurteilsfreien Dialog. Ein deutsch-deutscher Versuch. In Czyzewski *et al.* (eds), 203–31.

Ylönen S. 1991: Probleme deutsch-deutscher Kommunikation. Unterschiede im kommunikativen Verhalten zwischen Alt- und Neubundesbürgern. *Sprachreport* (2–3), 17–20.

Young, B. 1998: The strong German state and the weak feminist movements. *German Politics* 7(2), 128–50.

Zeh, W. (ed.) 1990: *Wegweiser Parlament*. Bonn: Bundeszentrale für politische Bildung.

Zimmer, M. 1997: Return of the Mittellage? The discourse of the centre in German foreign policy. *German Politics* 6(1), 22–38.

Zimmermann, H. 1985: *DDR Handbuch*. Köln: Wissenschaft und Politik.

Zohlnhöfer, R. 1999: Institutions, the CDU and policy change: explaining German economic policy in the 1980s. *German Politics* 8(3), 141–60.

Zurheide, J. 2000: Deutsch ist wichtiger als die eigene Muttersprache. *Der Tagesspiegel* 8 April, 4.

INDEX

Note: f. after a page number means
that page and the following
page; ff. after a page number
means that page and several
following pages.